FOOL ME ONCE

A Paige Taylor Mystery

BY KATHERINE E. KREUTER

Madwoman Press, Inc.
1994

This is a work of fiction. Any resemblance between characters in this book and actual persons, living or dead, is coincidental.

Cover by Phoenix Graphics, Winter Haven, Florida

Edited by Diane Benison and Catherine S. Stamps

Printed in the United States on acid-free paper

Library of Congress Cataloging-in-Publication Data

Kreuter, Katherine E., date.
    Fool me once : a Paige Taylor mystery / by Katherine E. Kreuter.
        p.   c.
    ISBN 0-9630822-8-0 (soft cover : acid-free) : $9.95
    1. Women detectives—United States—Fiction. 2. Women novelists, American—Fiction. 3. Lesbians—United States—Fiction. I. Title.
PS3561.R4637F66 1994
813′.54—dc20

                                                                                    94-32022
                                                                                        CIP

For
Karen Mayers

Acknowledgements

My thanks to Scott, Marilyn, Ann, both Moniques, and the sailors of the *China Doll* for their many contributions to this novel.

My gratitude to my editors, Diane and Catherine, for believing in the manuscript.

About the Author

Katherine E. Kreuter lives and writes in Southern California.

Prologue

In a purple rage, Sally Barrett stormed into the Pacific Palisades dental offices of Grimm and Barrett. Receptionist Alyce Maine, flushed from her chair like a quail, headed for cover in the ladies' room.

The lean, leggy, blonde beauty—if one's taste in women runs to lean, leggy blondes—sailed on. On past the two patients in the reception room, who instantly abandoned *People* and *Sports Illustrated* to stare mutely at this unexpected spectacle. On past the room where Dr. Frederick Grimm and his wife and dental assistant, Gretchen, were earnestly fitting a set of dentures into the gaping mouth of a patient.

At the end of the hallway, Sally flung open a door marked PRIVATE. Her husband, peeling off a pair of latex gloves messy from the first root canal of the day, jerked to attention.

Sally plunged her right hand into the side pocket of her purse and whipped out a piece of paper. Instant recognition of it added more exclamation points to Bill Barrett's eyes. Sally crushed it in her fist and fired the wad at him. Bill blinked reflexively and ducked, and the tiny missile flew by.

"You *rotten scum ball!*" screamed Sally. "I'm leaving you! For good! Do you *hear?*"

Bill Barrett heard. So did the numbed pair sitting in the waiting room and the shaken Alyce Maine, locked in the seclusion of the ladies' room. And so did Freddie and Gretchen Grimm, along with their helpless patient whose enormous blue eyes were fairly bulging out of their sockets.

"Sal, hey, please. Carole's dead now."

"So I should forgive and forget? Fuckit!"

"I'll make it up to you, Sal. I promise."

Bill reached out to her like the twisty saint extending his long limbs towards heaven in El Greco's painting of St. Francis receiving the stigmata. But hell, not heaven, answered his plea with a hard crack to the jaw. It left Bill speechless and running his tongue over his upper left molars, searching for damage. Sally, knuckle in mouth, bit back an enormous belly laugh as she spun on her heel and whooshed out of the office like a tidal wave on rewind.

Bill picked up the crumpled paper, put it in his pocket, pulled on a fresh pair of gloves and checked his watch. "Sweet Jesus," he whistled through his teeth. "Only eight fifty-five." He stepped gingerly down the corridor towards his second patient of the day.

"Outrageous," muttered Freddie Grimm. He exchanged covert glances with his wife, then headed thoughtfully towards the supply cabinet for a fresh tube of Polygrip.

O

The owner of the Tripout Travel Agency on Hollywood Boulevard faced Sally Barrett across his desk—a chaos of mail, tickets, shipping guides, airline schedules, the remains of a five-pound box of See's candy and an ashtray containing at least a dozen mauled butts of filter-tipped Salems.

"I want to go somewhere and disappear from the face of the earth," Sally told him. "Any suggestions?"

Sammy Bandini shifted in his chair. He got his share of crazies coming off the Boulevard, but none like this drama queen. He needed time to think. "Have a chocolate?" he asked.

Sally eyed the two creams remaining in the See's box and shook her head. She preferred nuts and chews. Something she could really sink her teeth into.

"Any suggestions?" she repeated. "How about a smart place with water? On the water."

"The Caribbean. That's it." Sammy reached for a buried cruise pamphlet.

"Been there."

Sammy stubbed out his cigarette with a series of left jabs to the filter. "Jeezz, this has really been a morning!"

Sally glanced at her watch. Nine forty-two already. How long was it going to take this fool? She drummed a red fingernail on the edge of Sammy's desk. "How about something high voltage?" she prompted.

Sammy stared at the flashing red nail and touched the flame of his lighter to a fresh Salem. "What about Beirut then? Or Belfast?"

"I like to create my own war zones," snapped Sally.

"Hunngh." Sammy hoisted his bulk into a standing position and moved it across the room to a large table where other pamphlets lay in a disorganized heap. He pawed through them, then picked one up and waved it in triumph.

"Alaska is out." Sally shook her head. It was time to spell it out for him. "I want something more exotic. You know, great shopping, international set, surprise cuisine."

Sammy dropped the pamphlet back onto the heap. "What about Hong Kong?"

"Hong Kong?" Sally's eyes brightened.

"Kicky place. On the water. Fantastic food. Great shopping." Sammy eyed the white Mercedes convertible Sally had left in the No Parking zone outside. "And *private* bank accounts, if you know what I mean." Her smile told him that she did indeed know what he meant. "International set. The jet set."

"Get set!" Sally laughed. "Sold. One-way to Hong Kong."
"One-way? How about stopovers? Honolulu, Seoul,
Tok—"
"No stopovers. Let's get there."
Sammy French-inhaled his Salem. "Let's get there," he
muttered, as he turned to his computer.

O

From her last stop, near the corner of Wilshire Boulevard
and Robertson, it took Sally exactly forty-four minutes to
drive the seventeen miles to Crestview Lane, a sleepy cul-de-
sac in posh Mandeville Canyon. She took advantage of the
time en route to carphone her hairdresser and cancel her
appointment for the following day. In a parking lot off Santa
Monica Boulevard, she stopped just long enough to open the
trunk, take out two empty briefcases, and toss them into a
dumpster.

Back in the driver's seat, Sally shoved a cassette of Act II
of Verdi's *Un Ballo in Maschera* into the stereo and, along
with Kiri Te Kanawa, belted out the windshield-rattling aria
'Ma dall'arrido stelo divulsa.'

It was almost noon when she pulled the Mercedes into the
three-car garage beneath the timber and adobe house she had
shared with Bill Barrett for nearly a year. She dropped the
Verdi cassette into her purse, stepped out of the car and
slammed the door. *"Ciao*, Baby!" she told it.

In the master suite upstairs, Sally undid her girlish ponytail and wove her blonde hair into an elegant French twist.
Then decorated her mulberry blouse with a weighty gold
necklace. Dangling between her breasts now was a sleek
golden dolphin, destined to leap forever through its diamond-
studded hoop. Sally smiled at her reflection in the bathroom
mirror and blew the dolphin a kiss.

From a walk-in closet she removed two jumbo burgundy suitcases and matching cosmetic case and quickly phoned for a taxi. Less than an hour later Sally was at Los Angeles International Airport and checked in on China Airlines' Flight 005 to Hong Kong, departing at three-fifteen. There was ample time for a stopover in the nearby cocktail lounge.

Reinforced by two very dry Stoli martinis, Sally was feeling quite in love with life in general and in particular quite proud of herself. "Really, I deserve an Oscar," she murmured, as she boarded the 747.

But the twenty-hour flight—with additional martinis and a delayed refueling stop in Taipei—left Sally with a bass-drum hangover. In the baggage claim area of Kai Tak Airport she finally succeeded in assembling her luggage on an airport cart. This, like so many of its ilk, had not only an independent mind and a nasty temper, but gravitational laws all its own.

With a final spurt of energy, Sally managed to thrust it through customs and immigration, on through the EXIT ONLY doors and out onto the wide ramp that led down into the greeting area. She searched the faces clustered at the far end. A pair of eyes locked with hers. Sally thrust both arms over her head in a triumphant **V** and shattered the air with the soprano shriek of a peacock.

O

I came on the scene about a week later.

Chapter One

From my nearly horizontal position in a dental chair, I exchanged a nod with Alyce Maine as she floated by the doorway, leaving a trail of Chanel Cristalle in her wake. I couldn't help but hear her melodious, "Dr. Barrett, your last patient of the day is waiting *patiently* for you" drift in a moment later from the end of the hall.

"Anyone I know?" Barrett began what sounded like a long drawn out yawn.

"New patient. Paige Taylor. Just a checkup and pro scale."

There followed something between a yelp and a snarl, which I took to be the termination of the yawn. But it sent a chill up my spine. When it comes to dentists, the coward in me takes over, body and soul.

My latest selection from the Yellow Pages was now filling the doorway. I hadn't much to look at but a standard-brands face with a close-cropped brown dome and clean-shaven slopes. And the kind of roving eyes that belong to a random sex trawler.

"I'm Dr. Barrett," he told the denim skirt that concealed about half of a pair of legs he obviously hoped to see in their entirety one day soon. Then he focused on what a Greek phenomenon named Melina used to call my Aegean-blue eyes and added, "You must be Paige Taylor."

"Yes, I suppose I must."

Barrett laid what I took to be my chart on the counter and reached for a probe and a mirror, but not without one last look that told me he was calculating my vital statistics. My guess was that he'd had plenty of practice and probably came up with about five foot seven and one hundred and thirty pounds. I closed my eyes and thought of England.

"How long has it been?" Barrett wanted to know as he began his dental inspection.

Since what? I felt like asking but squelched the impulse. I shrugged instead and listened to his stomach rumbling against my right ear. This immediate intimacy of dentist and patient always amazes me.

Click, click. Scrape, scrape. Great accompaniment for Barrett's chatter that ran its course like a B film, entertaining only because it looked silly moving in reverse: from tonight's Dodgers game all the way back through happy frat house college days to fast times at Pasadena High. Ballgames and girls. Fixated at sweet sixteen.

Barrett finally laid his mirror and explorer aside and glanced at the information on my chart. Halfway down the page, his eyes froze. "You're a private investigator?"

"Yes."

He lowered his spaniel eyes along with his voice. "I've been seriously considering...you see...my wife left me. Ten days ago." He snapped a rubber-gloved thumb and finger. "Just like that!"

The immediate intimacy of P.I. and prospective client still amazes me too. It was my turn to probe. "Disappeared?"

Barrett nodded. "My partner, Freddie Grimm, has been hounding me to hire a detective. He's convinced that Sally not only left town but left the country."

"What do you think?"

"Well, she did talk a lot about wanting to go around the world."

That got my attention fast. I'm curiosity's child, and travel is my passion.

Barrett folded his arms. "Anyway, I need a good man to track her down. Or better, a woman," he added. "You know... women think alike."

"I can assure you that I do *not* think like your wife," I shot back. "But that doesn't mean that I can't figure out what she thinks and what she's doing."

Barrett apologized, called himself thoughtless, and said he was exhausted from working and worrying about Sally. He pulled an instrument up to my cheek, then plopped a twenty-pound throw rug over my chest and said, "We need to take some X-rays. There are a couple of areas that look suspicious."

"I'm a gagger," I said sheepishly. "The fewer the better."

"No problem."

I tried to distract myself. "Tell me about Sally."

Barrett described her rage scene in his office. It was his turn to be sheepish. "Yes, I did have a little locket engraved for a friend," he admitted. "Sal found the bill."

How inconvenient. "Were there other women?"

"Well...Sally was, is, and always will be the...well, I guess Primary Person says it all."

Sure. "Had you known her long before you were married?"

"Just a few months. But the Grimms introduced us. Freddie and his wife Gretchen—GG. They arranged a blind date for us one weekend."

"Those can be fatal," I got out just before he stuck a large piece of cardboard in my mouth and maneuvered it up against my right molars. Gulgh.

"Bite down now," he instructed me.

I bit.

While he adjusted the X-ray machine, Barrett went on with his story. "Freddie rented a catamaran at Newport. He's a real nut for boats. Sal too. We sailed over to Catalina." He smiled at the memory. "Sunshine, sea air, bikinis and black Russians. There I was, a confirmed bachelor of forty, buzzed over some twenty-five-year-old I hardly knew. Don't move now."

He vanished through the doorway. The machine buzzed and clicked, and I spat out the cardboard as he returned.

"Almost a year ago now that Freddie and GG drove us to Vegas on Halloween weekend, and we tied the knot." Barrett stuck another piece of gag material in my mouth and shifted the X-ray machine. "It's been nothing but bad news lately. My receptionist drowned, the father of my next-door neighbor was murdered—right there in her backyard—and now Sally's gone." I gagged again. He said, "This is the last one."

The machine clicked and I got to my feet. I wanted out of there. Fast. "I'll be back for the results some other time."

"Fine with me," said Barrett. "Why don't we go somewhere and talk this Sally thing over?"

"Thanks, but not this evening. However, if you'd care to make an appointment with me?"

"How about tomorrow?"

"Saturday?" I took my pocket calendar from my purse and gave it a glance. "Around four?" Why not? After all, I was between cases.

"Great."

I took a card from my wallet and handed it to him. "My office is in my home. Castellammare Drive. If you're going west on Sunset..."

"I know. Just before I hit the beach I take a hard right."

"Up the hill and over above the coast highway. We're on the right. Old Spanish-style house. You'll see a black wrought iron stairway leading down to my office door." I replaced the calendar in my purse and took out my car keys. "But I can't promise to take the case. I'll need to know a good deal more about it."

"Of course."

I could feel his prowler's eyes trailing me out to reception, where I settled my account with Alyce Maine. I drove home thinking about my last case—the marriage dodger I followed across Russia on the Trans-Siberian Railway—and the novel it inspired: *Last Train to Tashkent*. I wondered what Barrett would inspire. Right now he was doing to my psyche what a hard bench does to my derrière.

Chapter Two

The next afternoon I stood looking out over the ocean from the turreted balcony of the bedroom I've slept in off and on since childhood. I was thinking about my parents, Marilyn Paige and Robert Taylor. They bought this house the year I was born, 1959, before prices skyrocketed, when a pair of young anthropologists could still afford the location. It's drop-dead gorgeous real estate, but it's the least of their legacy. My mother and father were inveterate travelers who dragged their only child everywhere from Mongolia to Madagascar. They gave me the ultimate course in Suitcase 101, a smattering of languages, and their passion for the ends of the earth—the same earth that swallowed them alive.

In the spring of my senior year at Berkeley they left for India and were never heard from again. That May I hired the Babcock Agency in San Francisco to track them, hopeful that they were merely lost to the world in one of the monasteries they had planned to visit. Babcock's detective made the rounds of the monasteries but drew a blank and returned to California a few weeks later, ten pounds thinner but no wiser. I panicked and bought a ticket for Calcutta. Early in June I collected my B.A. and my rucksack and said goodby to Berkeley.

Late that summer I discovered that my parents had been lost in an avalanche in Nepal, trying to scale Fish Tail Mountain. The way they would have wanted to go, I'm sure. They weren't the retirement types. But I wasn't ready to lose my two best friends. I sat in a little hotel in Pokhara and stared at the Himalayas. Finally one day I picked up a pen and began to write their story. It became my first novel.

When I got back to California I not only lucked out with a publisher, but the Babcock Agency began contacting me whenever it had some involvement with a missing person whose disappearance led abroad. That left me with twin professions—the pursuit of both fact and fiction. It also left me with an unexpected inheritance, two modest incomes and a house.

For the past seven years I've shared this house with my partner, Pat Towne. She's one of curiosity's children too, with a passion for travel that matches my own. She's my best friend, my pal, my love. My window on forever.

I was hoping that Pat would be home today in time to meet Barrett. She likes to see the faces that go with my cases. These she dives into with the same exhuberance she pours into her lectures at UCLA, where she's Professor of French and an old hand at shredding texts.

I read my watch and figured that by now Barrett would be taking the last curves on Sunset Boulevard as if the Indianapolis 500 had begun without him and he was already several laps behind. At least that's the way I visualized him—the kind that would peel rubber, too, alongside some other teenager.

I was wondering what kind of car he drove when a canary-yellow Corvette nosed up over the hill on Castellammare Drive, swerved to a stop next to our mailbox and parked. Barrett stepped out, sniffed the sea air, stopped to listen to the surf crashing against the beach below, then stepped briskly toward my office. Whatever he used for jock itch, I noted, didn't seem to be working.

It took me a minute to cross the bedroom, follow the wide corridor-cum-gallery to the terra cotta tile staircase that leads down to the living room, then another set of stairs on down to my office below. It was time enough for my assistant, Dick Kessler, to introduce himself and for Barrett to return a handshake and no doubt give his host a special smile of male bonding. Not an Achilles-Patroklos look, by any means. But one, nevertheless, that said here was an equal, rival or not.

I remembered the summer evening a half dozen years ago when Pat and I had gone to the open-air theater in Topanga Canyon and met Dick at the cast party afterward. He was still in his black fur leotard, a walk-on Dane in an avant-garde *Hamlet*. A walk-on Adonis now three years past thirty, terrified of middle age and a receding hairline, and of never finding Mr. Right.

Adonis was just about to buzz the intercom when I appeared in the doorway. He was wearing a chestnut tweed jacket that matched his well-groomed mustache and neck-length hair, a beige button-down shirt open at the throat, and immaculate cream slacks. He looked terrific. He always did.

After I greeted both men, Barrett and I sat down on the chocolate leather couch that stretched beneath a large Mark Rothko painting on the south wall. Dick was already behind his desk opposite us, pen and notebook in hand.

"Dr. Barrett—"

"Please call me Bill. And I want to say straight off that I read your X-rays and there's a tooth that looks like it could be trouble. You'll want to come in soon to get it fixed."

"I'll do that," I lied, and went right on with, "Bill, I've filled Dick in on your situation. How about giving us Sally's full name, and some background?"

Bill Barrett now leaned back into the couch and crossed his right ankle over his left knee. His lengthy narrative mode, apparently. "Sal grew up in Cicero—a Chicago suburb—as Leona Sally Romanski," he began. "Not a very happy childhood, I guess. But she made it through college on a scholar-

ship. Northwestern. Majored in Theater Arts. Sal spoke
French too. Spent a year at the Sorbonne."

"What kind of work did she do?"

"She auditioned for the New York City Ballet once. Didn't
make it. Said she didn't want to sleep with the choreogra-
pher."

"What else?"

"Well, Sal spent some time in San Francisco. Auditioned
for an opera there. Didn't make that one either. Too tall for
the tenor."

I tried catching Bill off guard: "Did Sally also take advantage of your open marriage?"

He stared at me with the eyes of an animal frozen in the
high beams of a car at night. "She never gave me any reason
to."

"Tell me who her friends are," I said.

"The two we saw most of were Freddie and GG, and they
both swear she never said a thing to them about leaving.
Freddie just talks about her bug to travel."

"Who else?"

"Oh, maybe half a dozen people in the L.A. area. But
nobody important. You know, like her hairdresser. The pool
man."

"What about neighbors?"

"Wouldn't have anything to do with them."

"Family?"

"Sal is an only child. Both her parents are dead. She said
she never wanted to see any of the relatives ever again. Guess
they took a dim view of her acting."

"What about friends around the country? Or abroad? Any
phone calls?"

Bill shook his head. "Sal didn't talk much about people.
Ask her about a play and she could tell you everything about
it. From Shakespeare to Simon, she knew theater."

"But no people?" I asked, trying to keep my tone neutral. He shook his head again. "Sal told me that first night on the boat, that her life had been really traumatic up until then. Up until me. Said she just didn't care to discuss it."

Didn't care to discuss it? My knee jerked at that one. That was Melina's favorite line, too. One I can do without.

"What else happened to Sally between college and marriage?"

"Well, there was Hollywood. She worked as an extra. She was between jobs when I met her."

"Extras are always between jobs," Dick muttered.

"Bill, are you telling us that you've paid Sally's way ever since?"

"Well, I guess so. If you want to put it that way."

"How would you put it?"

He gave me his caught-in-the-headlights stare again. "It was love. We fell in love."

This last 'love' was husky. Convincing. I asked, "Does Sally have her own checking account?"

"Yes, of course."

"What's the balance?"

"I don't know."

"Take a guess."

Bill took a long pause to rummage through some invisible figures on the north wall. "Probably in the neighborhood of ten grand."

"Enough for a little trip," I said. "Sally's apparently no stranger to travel."

"No. Not at all. Just last January we were in London for a dental convention, and she flew over to France for a few days."

"Where, exactly?"

"Paris—to pay her respects to the Sorbonne, she said. Take in some opera."

"Did you two do any other traveling during the past year?"

"No."

"Who's your travel agent?"

"Sunset Agency. Just a couple of doors from my office. I already asked if Sal had been in." Bill shook his head. "And she left her car in our garage."

"Doesn't leave me with much," I thought aloud. "Bill, how about telling us about the locket lady?"

His Adam's apple bobbed. "That was...Carole."

"She have a last name?"

"Oliver." The apple made a few more bobs. "You might have read about her—"

Dick jumped in with an animated, "About a month ago," and nodded in my direction. "Carole Oliver. Drowned. Body washed up under Redondo Beach Pier."

Dick is addicted to newspapers, particularly theater reviews and local gore. He says they have a lot in common. As an aspiring actor, he also has a tendency to make all the world his stage. I gave him a let-Bill-tell-it look.

"Carole lived in Redondo," Bill began. "She was quite a swimmer. But that night...well, police still think it was murder but haven't gotten anywhere. There were some bruises around her neck. They suspected me. I'd left a message on her phone machine." Bill stared at his shoes as if they might walk away without him. "Carole was my receptionist."

Dick's fist came down on his desk. "That's right! I remember now. Some dentist involved."

"I take it you had an alibi?" I asked Bill.

"I was in New York. Dental convention. Didn't get back until the next morning." Bill's foot tapped nervously to some melody only he could hear. "I left my car in a parking lot at LAX, but I lost my keys the last day of the convention. I phoned Sal from JFK. No answer. So I phoned Carole, got her machine. As it happened, I reached Sal later and she came and got me."

"Did Sally have an alibi?"

"She'd gone to a movie."

"Alone?"

"Alone."

I asked Bill for a little background on Carole. He said that they had met at the pool in his health club a few months after he had married Sally. Shortly afterwards, he hired her. He freely confessed that not long after that they began an affair. That was late February. Six months later she was history.

Bill shook his head. "What got me about Sal throwing that scene in my office, and making such a production of the bill for the locket, was that Carole had been dead for a month already!"

That sounded like a non sequitur to me, but I let it pass. He sounded like little-boy-lost when he asked, "Will you take the case?"

It didn't seem to have the smack of a *Last Train to Tashkent*, but then, that one got off to a slow start, too. Besides, I was really curious about Sally. She sounded much too exciting for Bill Barrett.

"Before you decide on me, you'd better have a look at my license." I picked up a folder from the table and handed it to Bill. "You may also wish to contact the Babcock Detective Agency in San Francisco to check my track record. Then think it over."

"I've thought it over." Bill returned the folder. "When I trust somebody, I trust them. Period."

Period? Spoken like the kind of guy who wins the javelin toss and elects to receive. I said, "I haven't told you my price."

Bill laughed. "Is it more than I charge?"

"No. But it's based on what you charge. I bill clients based on their incomes. I'll require a retainer, of course, and Dick will work out a payment plan with you."

"You've got a deal."

"Now," I said, "back to Sally. I'll need a list, with addresses and phone numbers, of anyone she has been in contact with in the last several months. And I'd like to see your house—her things. What about tomorrow?"

"Name your time."

"Two?"

"You got it."

"And I'll need to interview the Grimms. If they could drop by it would be helpful."

"No problem."

I got to my feet. "Now, how about something to drink to celebrate our arrangement?"

Bill must have been expecting the EJECT button. It took him a moment to respond, "Super!"

"Dick, check to see if Pat's home yet, will you?"

Dick picked up the intercom, waited a moment and then told it: "Ace McCool, requesting clearance for the bar.... No, I won't be joining you. Rehearsal tonight." He paused to give me a thumbs-up sign.

"Shall we?" I said to Bill.

Hugging my heels, he followed me up into the living room.

"Looks like some cult headquarters," he offered, surveying the assemblage of Oriental rugs and the water pipe sprawling in one corner. "Or a mosque."

His eyes narrowed as they began roving the walls, discovering everything from Greek steles to Pat's Klee and Kandinsky collection. In one corner they came to rest with a brief smirk on a life-size replica of a Khajurahan temple statue—a pair of blissful lovers. Of all the things I had dragged home from the four corners of the earth, this was my favorite.

Bill lost little time on the refectory dining table and the circular two-piece couch that embraced a low brass and silver coffee table in front of the fireplace. But lying across it was an object he was obviously having trouble with—all five feet of my sixteenth birthday present.

"It's a Brazilian bull-roarer," I told him. "Borobo tribesmen whirl it to make terrifying sounds. That keeps the women in the clan in their proper place."

My sarcasm was lost on him. He simply nodded and said, "Some cult!"

I couldn't wait until he saw the dusky goddess that the cult comes to worship. As a matter of fact, there she was now. Coming through the double doorway at the far end of the room.

Bill's appraisal began with the pair of greenest eyes—the very greenest—that he had ever, ever seen. Then lingered on ebony hair, falling softly in long waves onto bare shoulders. On dark-honey skin. On the hot pink sarong that gently molded what Bill had no doubt referred to as jugs at Pasadena High. His eyes bounced back and forth several times between the long flame earrings and lips that matched before circling on down to a wasp waist, luscious hips and bare feet that now came dancing toward him in what looked to me like a cross between a Hawaiian hula and a Cuban mambo.

I introduced Dr. Patricia Towne to Dr. William Barrett. Pat was on to him from minute one.

O

Getting ready for bed that evening, Pat and I were still mulling over my new case.

"Bill actually asked me where I met an auburn-haired P.I. like you" floated out of the shower.

"What did you tell him?"

"Told him I picked you up at a white sale."

That one put a clown's smile on my face. I pulled on a robe, stretched out on the bed and laced my fingers behind my head. "I'm waiting for you to deconstruct his text, as your academia nuts love to say. What's Sally up to?"

Pat's brief appearance in the bathroom doorway, stepping from the shower to the towel rack, evoked an involuntary sigh and redirected my thoughts.

"Sally's after something," she said, "but not Billy Barrett. He's HFH reality, something Sally would trade for illusion any day. For some real theater. High drama. A special effects man."

"HFH?" I asked.

"Ho Fuckin Hum. You should get around more."

I had to agree.

Pat reentered my field of vision, now wrapped in raspberry terrycloth. She was giving her hair its hundred strokes in front of her five-paneled mirror that looks to me like something out of a funhouse.

I said, "Sounds to me like Bill's words might not fit reality."

"Words, words, words," Pat repeated. "Language, as I like to tell nodding students, is like an ill-fitting girdle. It squeezes away one bulge only to reveal another."

I thought about that for one long moment. Until Pat had turned off the bathroom light and reappeared in the darkened doorway, wearing nothing now but her shimmering evening eyes.

"After an hour with you," I told the apparition, "Bill Barrett's probably suffering from a strange malaise now."

Pat leaned a hip against the doorframe and rolled her eyes heavenward, her version of a celestial vision. "Severe sensory deprivation?" she giggled.

A voice I hardly recognized as my own said, "Come here." Pat moved across the room as if she were walking on water. She bent over me and let her breasts stray across my lips. She untied the belt of my robe and slipped it away. And slowly, ever so slowly, she let her body sink into mine.

Chapter Three

Barefoot but still wearing shorts and a T-shirt from an early set of tennis with Pat, I was sprawled on the couch in my library, a fat pillow tucked under my head. I was on page twenty-seven of an Amanda Cross mystery, *The James Joyce Murder*. Just as Reed Amhearst began a rare outburst of obscenities, having stepped in an enormous mound of fresh cow dung, the intercom buzzed.

"It's one-fifteen, Madam, and you have a two o'clock appointment."

I glanced at my watch. "Thanks, Dick."

"Sure you haven't changed your mind about my going along?"

"No, don't bother. I'll fill you in later."

"Pat going with you?" Baritone laughter rumbled out of the wall.

"I doubt that she's in the mood for more of Bill's visual cannibalism."

"I heard that!" Pat threw open the double doors connecting my library to hers—two former adjoining bedrooms upstairs that we redesigned a few years ago.

"Has she solved the latest disappearance yet?" Dick teased.

"No, Mr. Kessler," Pat shot back, "but I'll give you your first clue."

"What's that?"

"Well, what do you add to a name like Leona Romanski?"

"How should I know?"

"Polish and Catholic."

"And?"

"And do Polish Catholics usually have just one child?"

I broke in with a laugh. "Not unless they're very, *very* sinful."

"And that puts us where?" asked Dick.

"In the same frame of mind," Pat answered, "as the Persian proverb which teaches that if a first building stone is askew, a structure may reach to the heavens, but it'll all be crooked."

Dick groaned. "That pretty well describes my last play. *The Three Sisters*, remember? When I stumbled on stage in the first scene, and all four acts turned into a quadruple nightmare?"

"Unforgettable," I murmured.

"Well, if you don't need me, I'll split for the beach and a jog," he said. "Do we rendezvous later?"

"How does five o'clock sound?"

"Like the cocktail hour."

"Meanwhile, sorry to ask, but how about seeing what you can get on Carole Oliver?"

"It's Sunday."

"I knew that."

I heard a "Hungh!" before Dick clicked off the intercom. I turned to the arms-folded figure now posed in the doorway like Socrates on an all-night meditational. "Polish and Catholic, huh?" I pried myself off the couch. "I'll give that some thought while I slip into something less comfortable."

"For Billy Boy? How about a coat of mail?" Pat suggested, making an Italian gesture involving her left hand and the crook of her right arm. "Over a chastity belt."

I headed for the shower.

○

I drove leisurely along Sunset Boulevard, enjoying the autumn breeze with the top down on my Jaguar. It's a cream-colored 1982 that I bought with royalties from my Himalayan saga, have taken tender care of ever since, and will probably never part with. I like that close-to-the-earth feeling it gives me.

I pointed it north up into Mandeville Canyon, and several minutes later dipped down into Crestview Lane. It looked to me like some cul-de-sac Fantasy Island. With all the trees and shrubbery, I could barely make out one English country cottage, two Hawaiian ranch houses, a glassy imitation Frank Lloyd Wright and a New Mexican adobe and timber. In front of this a mailbox read 1448.

I pulled to the curb, parked and stepped out. Before I had even reached the sidewalk, Bill Barrett flew out of the front door as if chased by a swarm of bees.

"This was all I needed. Try to be a good neighbor and take care of their dumb Daffodil while they go to Phoenix and that damned dachshund gets into the wastepaper basket in our bathroom and eats a pair of pantyhose Sal tossed out before she left."

I decided against a comment on the appetitive pantyhose and said, "Take it easy, Bill. No need for hysterics."

"So I go to the vet's. Daffy's stomach's blocked—"

"Is she all right now?"

"It's still touch and go. What in hell am I going to tell my neighbors when they get home tonight?"

"We'll figure something out." I took his elbow and steered him towards the front door. "How about inviting me in?"

Bill held the door, then followed me into the atrium. I tried bringing him back to the here-and-now. "Why don't I have a look at the backyard first? I like to start with the outside and work my way in."

That prompted a wink and a suggestive "Me too" from Bill. I mentally kicked myself for giving him an opening.

I followed him down a corridor that led to the back door and out into the patio. A kidney shaped pool bordered with slate decking was the main attraction. A couple of pink-cushioned lounge chairs rested on the surrounding grass. Beyond that, beds of petunias alternated with rose bushes along the three sections of six-foot beige cement wall that marked the property line. Over it, to the west, a corner of the roof of the Hawaiian ranch house next door poked through a tangle of olive branches.

Bill's eyes trailed mine. "Daffy's house."

I said, "I thought you and Sally didn't mingle with the neighbors."

"Well, Sal didn't. But I had one of those over-the-back-fence conversations with them, and next thing you know they're calling me their new dentist."

"Who are we talking about?"

"Silvia Mandariaga. And her friend—her housekeeper, I guess—Elena."

"Mandariaga rings a bell."

"Silvia is a violinist with the L.A. Philharmonic."

"I don't make a connection there."

"Her father was a classical guitarist."

"Yes, that's it. Manuel Mandariaga. So he's the one you mentioned to me in your office. I didn't know he had died."

Bill gave me a vague nod.

I said, "You have something on your mind."

"It happened while he was visiting here. Silvia was playing a concert in San Francisco, Elena had gone up there with her. Manuel had stayed home. He was in his eighties, you know."

"Heart attack?"

"Murder. Burglary and murder. But the burglary looked faked. They found Manuel on the back steps. Whoever did it beat the old man bloody."

I shuddered, and made a mental note to ask Dick about it. "Let's go back inside," I said, wanting to refocus Bill's thoughts on Sally.

A tour of the ground floor netted me a pleasant display of contemporary, comfortable furniture, but I couldn't detect Sally's presence anywhere. It was all so impersonal.

Bill and I headed upstairs for an exploration of the second floor. In the bathroom of the master suite, he pointed out the wastepaper basket where the ill-fated pantyhose had been abandoned, and I searched the remainder of the room. Besides an emptied jewelry box and a few scattered cosmetics left by a woman who spent a good deal of time on herself, it revealed little of interest. Not a clue about where that woman might have gone.

The closets were barren of clues too. I ran one finger across a row of empty hangers. Pink and padded. "Nice," I said to Bill.

He followed me over to the dresser. "That's some house you have."

"Thank you." I opened a drawer.

"And Dick lives downstairs, huh?"

"That's right."

"And Pat's really a professor of French at UCLA?"

"That is correct. She really is."

"I suppose she's Hawaiian. Or maybe has some Tahitian blood?"

"No. African-American. Black." I closed the bottom dresser drawer.

"Black?" he repeated. "She's not black."

"Pat Towne is black. Her father is black. Her mother is the daughter of a white man and a black woman. That makes Pat black."

"She's part white then."

I instantly regretted asking, "Which part?" Bill's raucous laugh told me his libido had resurfaced.

I moved into the next room. It contained nothing more than an exercise bicycle and an armless chair behind a dainty oval desk.

"Do you have the key to this desk?" I asked, when none of the drawers responded to my tugs.

"Key?"

Did I imagine it, or did panic flicker in his eyes?

"Oh, key. Yes. Key." Bill's right hand rummaged in the desk organizer and came up victorious.

I went through each drawer, scanned the household bills and bank statements, noted without interest the usual supplies of envelopes, paper, pens, rubber bands, paper clips and a tube of super glue.

"Sally managed the household?"

"Sure did. I never had to worry about a thing."

"You trusted her completely?"

That brought on his first blinded-by-the-car-lights stare of the day.

"Wouldn't have gotten married if I hadn't," he finally answered. "So I'm an old-fashioned guy—"

"No pre-nuptial contract?"

"No way," said Bill. "I'm an all-or-nothing-at-all type. I throw it all in. Take it or leave it. I mean, if I couldn't trust my wife like I trust my own mother, I wouldn't get married."

I was surprised he didn't add, "Period." I picked a few twenty-nine-cent stamps out of a small tray and was about to replace them when I noticed something of a different color stuck to the bottom of one of them.

"Well, a fifty-cent stamp!"

I looked up. My guess was that Bill would study a puzzling cavity the same way he was studying the stamp.

"Nobody keeps fifty-cent stamps on hand unless they have correspondance with someone abroad," I said. "And you say Sally never wrote to anyone outside the States?"

"No," he answered as the doorbell rang.

"Not that you know of, that is."

Bill headed downstairs to answer the door. I called after him, "Did Sally write for reservations for you in London?"

"No. The conference coordinator took care of everything."

"What about Paris?"

"Said she didn't need a reservation. Said she'd just find something on the spot."

"Where did she stay?"

"Somewhere in the Latin Quarter."

"Do you remember a hotel name?"

"I don't think she ever gave me a name, but she did say it was in some street called...something about the heart...or heartbeat. Street where the heart lies. I think that was it. She said lots of streets in Paris have crazy names."

I found myself humming *April in Paris* as I continued my inspection of the second floor. Two guest rooms and another bathroom. All surprisingly impersonal—like the downstairs. Something of a model house decorated by Rodeo Drive boutiques for wealthy transients. I headed down the stairs, wondering what on earth had attracted Sally to Bill Barrett and induced her to give up a career in the theater.

The Grimms were with Bill in the sunken living room. Following introductions, the four of us sat down on the lavender playpen assemblage facing the slate fireplace. Freddie and Gretchen were cooperative, but he did most of the talking, letting his dark manipulative Daniel Day-Lewis eyes rest mainly on mine. He was an attractive man, fortyish, with thick black hair and lots of spark. In contrast to Bill's pale skin and straight-arrow outfits of darkish trousers and light shirts, Freddie sported crisp white slacks and a teal polo shirt that decorated nicely suntanned biceps.

GG was one of those women who adore their men. She probably had from the first moment they had met, at Long Beach State College. Freddie had just completed a bachelor's degree in pre-dentistry and she a dental assistant program. They fell in love and married, after which GG worked in a Palos Verdes dental office and put her husband through dental school at USC. That's where he met Bill.

I found myself making a mental note on how to describe Gretchen Grimm in some future novel. She had sheenless salt and pepper hair, with a black barrette pulling one side up a bit higher than the other. Above a dull face. Dutiful but dull.

So what did Freddie see in her? I began speculating about their sex life, but cut that little spree short. I hate myself when I start that. Probably because I don't want anybody speculating about mine.

"How about a drink?" Bill got to his feet. "I make the best Stoli martinis in the canyon, as some of you already know."

Yes, the three of us would welcome martinis. Bill crossed the room to the wet bar.

I turned to the Grimms. "I understand you met Sally just a few months before you introduced her to our bartender?"

"Yes," Freddie continued as spokesperson. "It was a party in connection with an opening at The Music Center. People...you know...mingle...introduce themselves. We thought right away, didn't we GG, that Sal and Bill would blend—"

"Like Stoli and vermouth," came the voice from behind the wet bar.

"We decided we should get to know her a little first," Freddie went on, "so we got together now and then. A dinner here. A play there."

I asked, "Was she ever with anyone?"

"No."

"Did she ever mention any of her other friends?"

"No." Freddie looked at GG, and she shook her head.

"Family?"

The Grimms shook their heads again.

"Her past?"

"I guess Sal's favorite tense is the present," Freddie said. "She's a pretty private person." He cracked his knuckles a couple of times before he went on with: "I'd say Sally has two loves. Travel and the theater." GG nodded agreement. "So one day we asked her if she'd like to go sailing."

Bill laughed. "And chemistry did the rest." He was crossing the room again, this time with a tray of martinis.

O

Two hours later I was curled up between two rosy cushions on the couch in my own living room, with Dick sprawled next to me. Pat was in the kitchen, eavesdropping, and preparing paella with her usual flair. Pat can stir soup with a reggae beat that makes your feet twitch, and when she whips up an omelette it sounds like a five-piece steel-drum band.

Dick filled me in on his conversation with a Lieutenant Bashore, who had investigated Carole Oliver's death. Carole was a former swimsuit model, a middle-aged brunette clinging to a string of "gentlemen callers," as Dick put it in his vocabulary-of-the-day. I suspected he had been reading *The Glass Menagerie*.

According to the lieutenant, the autopsy performed on Carole's body had shown puzzling traces of chlorine. But he later discovered that she had spent most of that final afternoon at her gym. Two of the regulars had seen her in the pool. Dick concluded with: "No concrete motive for murder and no suspect. Case closed."

"Speaking of cases," I said, "I suppose you read about the Mandariaga murder?"

"Are you kidding? Brutal."

"Your memory amazes me."

"It wasn't that long ago."

"Like when?"

"Maybe a month or so. Why?"

"Bill mentioned it this afternoon. Showed me the scene of the crime. Next door."

"Whoa!" Dick sniffed and twitched his mustache. "Did Bill tell you the old man was bludgeoned to death?"

"More or less."

"With a cast-iron Madonna?"

"A what?"

"There was a little shrine in the garden, with a metal statue of the Virgin Mary."

I was still staring at Dick when he added, "You should read the papers."

"Why should I? I have you."

Dick shrugged.

"Find out the date of death, yes?"

"Yes."

I switched to my own afternoon. My report of the "street where the heart lies" verified that Pat was eavesdropping.

"Rue Gît-le-coeur," she called out. "A narrow little street. One short block. A Pizza Pino at one end, the Seine at the other. Two or three little hotels. Fodor's would be polite and list them as inexpensive."

"So why would Sally stay there?" Dick wondered.

"For nostalgic reasons, maybe?" came from the kitchen.

I said, "Sally certainly didn't leave much on Crestview Lane to feel nostalgic about. Some clothes. A few dozen old cassettes. Bill said she brought very little with her when they married. Said she wanted all new things for an all new life."

"Get real, Bill!" Pat sang out from the kitchen.

"Sally must have stashed her things somewhere," Dick said. "That fifty-cent stamp makes me wonder if she was in touch with someone abroad. Someone she didn't want Bill to know about."

"She'd have to pick up mail somewhere. Like at a post office box."

"And probably close by," I added. "Somewhere not far out of her way."

"Convenient." Dick nodded. "Because if anyone was going to bother to find it, the location wouldn't matter."

"I doubt very much that she would put the box in the name of either Barrett or Romanski, but a clerk might recognize her. She probably bought stamps and things there, too." I took an envelope from my briefcase. "I borrowed some photos from Bill."

Pat abandoned her saffron and rice and waltzed into the living room. "And so the plot sickens, as I am often prompted to add to an exposition," she commented as she peered over my shoulder at the pictures.

I narrated them. Sally, wearing clam diggers, leaning against her new Mercedes; Sally in a coral thong bikini draped on the deck of a sailboat, and at the helm, in the background, in navy-blue Speedo trunks and a skipper's cap, Freddie; the Grimms and Barretts in formal attire in a Las Vegas chapel.

"Love this one!" I held up a last picture of the quartet at the wedding dinner. In Halloween costumes. Bill in a frog suit, Freddie as Hamlet, Sally as Cinderella at the ball, and GG looking rather like Cinderella before the ball. I replaced them in the envelope and handed it to Dick. "First thing tomorrow, start making the rounds of the local post offices."

"I was afraid you were going to say that." Dick sniffed and twitched his mustache again. "What do I tell them?"

"You'll dream up something clever," I said. "Think of it as your chance for an Oscar."

O

Pat and I had cleared the patio table of dinner dishes and were heading for the living room and coffee.

"Suppose it's cool enough to light a fire?" she suggested as much as asked.

"Why not? If it gets too hot we can always strip."

"That's what I like about you," Pat giggled. "Your instant alternate plans for any situation. Makes you deliciously unpredictable."

"As unpredictable as Carole Oliver?" I wondered aloud.

"Who says she was? I don't buy her random decision to go for an evening swim. Tell me why she'd spend the afternoon gulping pool water at her gym and then head out to sea at night."

I lip-synced yes.

"Random," Pat repeated, and I could see her thoughts were spiralling inward. "Like the modern novel," she went on, drifting off into academese, "it's the aleatory that's really alluring. The random. In fact, that's the thread that stitches it to modern physics. The point I'm trying to make in the Samuel Beckett paper I'm working on for the Paris conference."

"Sweetheart," I said, "how about getting your manuscript while I fix a fire? We'll curl up on the couch and you can read it to me."

"So you want a preview of coming attractions?"

"When is it we leave for Paris? The twenty-fourth?"

"Eeeek! I'll never be ready!" Pat gave me a look streaked with Edvard Munch horror. "Besides, I am *sick* of this paper. It's so condensed now, it's unintelligible!" She headed upstairs for her library, then suddenly turned around. "By the way, I've been meaning to ask you all evening. How can you *possibly* stand working for Billy Barrett? For all his professional expertise, he's still the kind of geek who would think a dipthong is some kind of skimpy bathing suit."

I looked upward and into the distance, gazing at an imaginary Mount Everest. "I just think of myself as atop tall buildings," I told her.

The intercom buzzed, interrupting my scene. "Now hear this," said Dick, probably using his fist as a bullhorn and sounding rather like the captain of a doomed submarine. "Manuel Mandariaga was murdered the same night that Carole Oliver died."

I looked at Pat. All she said was, "That reminds me of the title of my paper."

I let my eyebrows ask the Which is? question.

"Autism for Two."

Autism?

Chapter Four

"Good Monday morning. Westwood Hairstyles. Twinka speaking."

"Twinka?"

"That's right."

"I like your name."

"Most people do."

"It suits your twinkly voice."

"Why, thank you. Hey, who is this?"

"My name is Paige."

"Like in a book?"

I laughed. "Close enough."

"What can I do for you?"

"I'm trying to get in touch with one of your clients. Sally Barrett. Would you by chance be her hairstylist?"

"I am. She would have no one but Twinka do her hair."

"It may surprise you then that Sally has disappeared, and her husband, Bill Barrett, whom you may have met—"

"The jerk."

"Has asked me to find her."

"You a friend of his or what?"

"Private investigator. We're concerned that she may do something foolish. Or even dangerous."

"To herself? Are you kidding?" Twinka shattered my ear with a screech. "Not Sally. Not the type."

"No? What type is she?"

Another screech. "Fast lane. Fun and games."

I thought a moment. "I wonder if you could tell me the date of her last appointment, Twinka? I'd really appreciate it."

"I guess so. Hold on...." Pages fluttered. "The twenty-sixth."

"Of September?"

"Yeah. But she called that morning and canceled it. All her regular Friday afternoon appointments, as a matter of fact. Said she'd be in touch." Papers rattled. "You don't really think she's in a jam, do you?"

"Did she often cancel appointments?"

"Only if she was going away on a trip."

"Did she say anything about a trip this time?"

"Nope. Just said she'd be in touch. Haven't heard a word since. Must be some trip!"

I held the phone a few inches from my ear to minimize the effects of a third screech before I said, "Would you mind checking your records to see if Sally missed an appointment in January? I believe she went abroad."

"Yeah, I know she did. Raved on and on about Paris when she got back. Let's see here.... January 13."

"Anything for February? March?"

"Nope."

"What about April?" There was a long pause. "Hello?"

"I'm looking, I'm looking. Nope. Nothing until...yeah, thought I remembered that. Extra one in August. Something special."

"Not a trip to New York?" I ventured.

"The jerk went to New York. I remember Sally telling me that. She stayed home. Sick of him is my guess. But next appointment here, she's wearing this great piece o' jewelry, like a gold dolphin and a hoop o' diamonds. Zap your eyes out. One happy lady, she was! My favorite client, too."

"Were there any other cancellations, Twinka? Before September?"

"Nope." Another screech preceeded: "Crazy lady!"

"Crazy?"

"Decided to see if brunettes had more fun!"

"Brunettes?"

"That was May. Looked good, too."

"You changed her hair color?"

"She was back here the same day, tired of it already. So back to blonde we went."

I paused. "Well, what's your guess? Where is Sally?"

"Somewhere where the action is."

"Twinka, I really appreciate your help. Perhaps I can return the favor—"

"Stop by one day. You might like my style."

"I'm sure I would."

I replaced the receiver in its cradle and went over to the large globe that sat on an oak stand in one corner of my library. Eyes closed, I spun it around and let my finger come randomly to rest. When I looked again, it was occupying northern Chad. No, I was thinking when the phone rang, Chad is definitely not Sally's kind of action.

I was surprised to hear Bill's voice. "I may have another client for you," he said. "I was just talking with Silvia Mandariaga. She'd really like to meet you. Any chance you're free later? You could stop by here and I'd introduce you."

"Aren't you in the office today?"

"Monday's my day off. Freddie takes Saturday. That way we're open six days a week. One of Freddie's smarter ideas."

"I'd like very much to meet Ms. Mandariaga," I said. "How would early afternoon be? Say around two?"

"Super. I'll touch base with her. If you don't hear from me in the next few minutes, we're on."

"See you then."

I went into the kitchen and fixed a cup of cappuccino. Took it back to the library and sat down again at my desk. "Chad," I muttered.

My eyes wandered over the vertical bookshelves and horizontal map shelves that filled the three windowless walls. Then focused again on the sheet of paper before me—Bill's list of names, addresses and phone numbers. They had all been checked off and, with the exception of Westwood Hairstyles, had contributed no information of value.

I opened a telephone directory and began calling the taxi companies in the yellow pages. I was lucky. The sixth one I called, U-Needa-Cab, had a record of a Mrs. Barrett picked up on September 26 on Crestview Lane and delivered to Los Angeles International Airport. I asked if they would please locate the driver and have him call me back.

I had just finished my cappuccino when the phone rang again.

"This is Dick."

"Dick? Which Dick?"

A long pause.

"The driver Dick."

"Oh, sorry. I thought it was my Dick."

"Beg pardon?"

"My Dick. That is, my assistant Dick."

Another long pause.

"Huh?"

"Dick, my name is Paige, and I wonder if you recall taking a Mrs. Barrett from Mandeville Canyon to LAX on September 26?"

"Sure. Couldn't forget that broad."

"Do you remember where you dropped her off? Which airline?"

"Uh...United, maybe. Yeah, I think it was United. Well, no, maybe not. Uh...then again, it might have been Northwest. Or...I dunno."

"Did she say where she was going?"

"Huhunh. And I didn't ask. Wacko lady, singin' all the way down the freeway. Sounded like some kinda opera."

"Thank you, Dick. Let me give you my phone number in case you remember something later on. It's really important."

Calls to United and Northwest proved fruitless. I opened the Paris Hotel Guide Pat had left on my desk and flipped to the Sixth Arrondissement section. A few phone calls later I knew that none of the hotels on Rue Gît-le-coeur had any record of a Madame Barrett in January.

I walked over to the globe again and spun it. My finger came to rest on the Panama Canal.

"*Merde!*" I said aloud.

○

Just as I was parking my Jag by the mailbox at 1448 Crestview Lane, Bill Barrett burst through the front doorway and lurched down the sidewalk towards me. The same swarm of bees are after him, I thought. Only today there are more of them.

"The Krugerrands!" he yelped. "The Krugerrands are gone! All of them!"

"All right, Bill. Easy."

"All the Krugerrands! They're all—"

"Let's chill this."

I quickly escorted him inside and over to the the lavender playpen. "Sit down and tell me what this is all about."

Bill sat, tilted his head back and closed his eyes tightly. Then he took a deep breath, snorted, opened his eyes again, and gave me a Death Row look.

"The Krugerrands. They were in the safe. All of them."

"How much are we talking about?"

"Well over half a million dollars."

"Let's go see the safe."

I followed him upstairs and into the corridor leading to the master bedroom. He took a large seascape painting down from the wall and threw open the heavy metal door it had concealed.

"See what I mean? They're all gone! Every last—"

"Yes, I see. When did you discover this?"

"Just now. I had put some insurance papers in here and went to get them. Oh, the papers were there all right, but—"

I couldn't believe my ears. "Don't tell me you haven't opened the safe since Sally's disappearance!"

"No." Bill sounded as if he could hardly believe it himself. "I rarely use it. Have another one at the office. All we put in here generally were the Krugerrands. We'd only open it to add to 'our little stash,' as Sally called it. 'Our little secret.'"

"Whose idea were they?"

"Ours, of course." Bill paused to reconsider this. "Well, Sally, I guess, suggested them in the first place. 'Good as gold,' she'd giggle. 'Good as gold.' I can still hear her. She had about nine thousand reasons why gold was the only way to go."

"Give me a few?"

"Well, things like they're better than American Eagles or Maple Leafs because they're harder. You know, better for currency. 'They're the only real universal currency,' she'd say. 'Good anywhere in the world. Anytime. And they don't leave a paper trail, like dollars. No serial numbers. Nobody can trace a Krugerrand.'"

"Let's hope we can trace Sally."

"Why, I trusted her like I trust my own mother!"

"You've told me that," I said quietly. "Where did the money come from?"

"Come from?" Bill stared at me, dumbfounded. "Come from? For Chrissakes! They're my life's savings! Nearly fifteen years of work there. Root canals, plates, extractions, crowns—"

"Is the house in joint tenancy?"

"This place? No. We lease it." Bill's voice was thinning. "The Krugerrands were the bulk of it. When we got married I sold the house I had in Santa Monica Canyon and bought Kru—"

"Any other assets?"

"Some stocks. Not much. Half of the business, of course."

"Savings accounts?"

"No. Every time I'd get a chunk ahead we'd buy Kru—"

"The cars?"

"Corvette's mine. Mercedes is leased."

"You do have your own checking account?"

"Yes."

"How much?"

"Maybe a few thousand." Bill's eyes drooped from spaniel to bloodhound. For a moment I thought he was going to cry.

"Looks like Sally got off with more gold than a dolphin necklace," I murmured.

"Dolphin?" Bill gave me his caught-in-headlights stare again. "Sal never had any dolphin necklace."

"She didn't?"

O

It was nearly three o'clock before Bill had pulled himself together and we walked next door. Silvia Mandariaga and Elena Sandoval were waiting for us. I liked them immediately. Warm and quiet-spoken. With a soft, savory Andalusian accent. I guessed fiftysomething. Very little grey in their straight black hair, which Silvia wore short and Elena long, pulled tightly away from her face and wound into an aristocratic chignon. Elegant hands, both of them. And with dark eyes that sent "Blue Spanish Eyes" singing through my mind. The looks those eyes exchanged told me that these women were more than friends.

Their home became them; it was a rich tapestry of the full lives they obviously led. The rooms resounded with music. Impressive sound system, white Gaveau piano, a wall lined with two guitars, a trio of violins, a balalaika and a mandolin.

I looked at them, thought of my own guitar, and sighed. "My first love was music," slipped out of me. "I often regret not having tried to make a career of it."

Elena smiled. "I too."

"But Elena is an excellent pianist," said Silvia. "Quite an accomplished musician."

Elena added, "Nothing compared with Silvia and Manuel."

"Well, I'm afraid I'm nothing compared with my father," Silvia told me. "He thought second violin with the L.A. Philharmonic reeked of failure."

"Unfair," I said.

"Not to father, I'm afraid. But we disagreed on most everything. We argued constantly."

Somehow I couldn't imagine Silvia arguing. My guess was that Manuel knew how to push her buttons.

Silvia said, "The police even suspected me of his murder."

"But you were in San Francisco."

"They suggested that I hired the job done. That it was made to look like burglars were taken by surprise."

I said, "Did they also suggest a motive?"

"The inheritance."

Silvia's eyes drifted to the photograph on the buffet. She and Elena, with Manuel Mandariaga in the center. He towered over Elena and a few inches over his daughter. Silver hair and goatee. And the same dark blue Spanish eyes that started the song on a rerun through my mind.

"I want to know who murdered him," said Silvia. "And why. If the police don't come up with a lead soon, we're going to hire a private detective. Bill suggested you."

"This isn't my usual kind of case." I stared at the photo and thought of Manuel's long slender fingers and their elegant performances. "But," I added, "somehow my heart is in this."

That seemed to bring Bill out of his Krugerrand coma. He smiled approval.

"Would you like to tell me what the police found?" I asked.

Silvia gestured to the front door. "This was pried open, the house turned upside down, some jewelry and cash taken, but very little."

Elena made an effort to smile. "We kept most of our treasures in shoe boxes and such."

"The police figured that burglars would have cased the house, known that Elena and I were gone, thought no one was home. You see, Daffodil doesn't bark." Silvia's hands began to tremble when she said, "My father was perhaps in the back yard. And heard some noise. Would you come with me, please?"

We trooped after her, through the dining room, kitchen and out the rear door. Down three steps to the patio floor.

"My father was probably coming in to investigate when the burglar—or imitation burglar—connected with him here." Silvia indicated the steps. "This is where the gardener found him early the next morning."

I looked around the yard. No pool. It had a well-mani-cured plot of grass, an assortment of shrubs and some olive trees. In the east corner there was a shrine—a clay replica of a mission church, about three feet high, and to one side, a cast-iron Madonna. "The murder weapon," I murmured. I looked at Silvia. She was on the edge of tears.

She said, "We didn't know what to do with it."

Well, I wouldn't either. I walked over to a bed of daffodils to give her time to breathe.

Elena turned to Bill. "Daffy's doing quite well today," she said. "We're to pick her up this afternoon."

Bill took a deep breath and blew it out slowly.

○

I had just closed the front door and walked into my library when I heard Dick's Harley Davidson streak up Castellammare Drive and skid into the garage. I pressed the intercom button.

Dick answered with a breathless, "I found it!"

"Get your biscuits up here. On the double!"

When he sailed through the doorway seconds later, he threw his arms wide and gave me a baritone "Ta-*da!*" No doubt about it—nothing Dick loves better than a grand entrance.

"I took a map and a compass," he began. "Put the point at 1448 Crestview Lane, drew a circle with a ten-mile radius, then marked all the post offices on it. And sure enough— Brentwood! Easy fifteen-minute drive for her."

"Bravo!" I said from the wet bar, where I was mixing margaritas.

"They had no record of a Barrett or Romanski," he went on. "So I show the photos to this one burly guy, and I can see right away he recognizes her. Grabbed the bikini shot right out of my hand! But of course he wants to know why I don't know her name. And I tell him I *do* know her name, but this isn't it. Like, I'm Dick Barrett, her brother, and our father has had a fatal accident—suicide, actually. And although my sister hated him—that's why she got the secret P.O. box in another name—she would want to hear from me now."

"What a moronic series of non sequiturs!" I couldn't help saying. "And he bought *that*?"

"You should have been there. Was I convincing! If I can just be that convincing tonight."

"What's tonight?"

"My audition." Dick read his watch. "Have to leave here in half an hour."

I filled two glasses, handed one to Dick and we settled down on a couple of barstools.

"Did you get the name Sally used for the P.O. box?"

"Lee Roman. I also found out that she canceled it."

"When?"

"He wouldn't say. Or when she got it, either."

"Maybe I'll work on him tomorrow. The dates could really be important."

"I'll go back and pump him more if you want."

"No, you won't have time."

"I won't? May I ask why?"

"You're going to Chicago."

"Chicago?" Dick bellowed as Pat opened the front door. She said, "No. It's Pat. Pat Towne. I live here."

I held up my glass. "Margarita?"

Pat dropped her purse and briefcase by the door. "Just pass me the Tequila bottle," was her answer.

"Bad Day at Black Rock?"

"Department meeting."

"Same thing." I poured a third margarita and took it over to the boneless body now flung onto the couch.

It asked meekly, "Is my glue showing?"

"Not if you keep your wings folded."

Dick repeated, "Chicago?"

"Yes." I settled back onto the barstool. "See if you can dig up a Romanski or two in Cicero. See what they have to say about Sally. I think she's full of surprises. This morning Bill Barrett discovered the house safe emptied of over half a million in Krugerrands."

"Eeeeeee!" came from Dick.

"So much for liquid assets." Pat peered into the foamy bubbles of her margarita. "So liquid that they just went down the drain."

Her timing was treacherous. With his throat full of his own bubbles, Dick nearly choked.

"And I have more," I said. "I met Silvia Mandariaga today, and her companion Elena Sandoval. Silvia's thinking about hiring a private eye to find her father's murderer. Bill recommended me."

"Hey, fantastic!" came from Dick. "But let's talk Chicago. What if I get the part tonight?"

"Don't worry, you'll be back in time for rehearsals." I reached for an envelope in my briefcase. "I'll drive you to LAX in the morning and fill you in on the details en route. We should leave the house at six."

"Six? You must be kidding!"

"Must I?" I handed him the American Airlines envelope.

"Six," Dick muttered as he put his empty glass on the bar and headed for the downstairs door.

"Whoa," I called after him. "Where are you auditioning tonight?"

"I thought you'd never ask." Dick twitched his mustache and sniffed. "It's a private high school. Catholic girls' school, actually."

"And they're importing males?"

"Only the very best."

"Dare I ask what play?"

"Would you believe *Pride and Prejudice*?"

"*Pride and Prejudice*," Pat repeated. "Oh, do let me guess which part." She rolled her eyes to the ceiling and swooned. "Mr. Darcy!"

Dick beamed. "Who else?"

Chapter Five

In my seat by the front door of Tripout Travel, I watched Sammy Bandini consume two boxes of Raisinettes and smoke four Salem cigarettes down to their filter tips. All of the above while he booked an elderly couple on a sixteen-day castle tour of the British Isles.

Sammy escorted the glazed pair out the door. "Thirty-three castles in all," he wheezed at me. "More than two a day!"

I smiled, suspecting that the three and thirty would all coagulate in their memory by day seventeen.

"Come on over to my desk." Sammy hauled his hulk across the room. "Boy, has this been another one of *those* days!"

Did he ever have any other kind?

Sammy pulled open a desk drawer and found another box of Raisinettes. "Want some?"

"No, thanks."

"So what can I do for you?"

"I'd like a one-way ticket to Hong Kong."

"Holy Mother of God, another one! Gonna drive me bananas!" Sammy reached for a fresh Salem. "Jesus, what is going on in Hong Kong, anyway? Woman in here a coupla weeks ago, same thing. One-way. Hong Kong."

"Oh?"

"And I don't even like to sell one-way tickets. Usually refuse, as a matter of fact."

"Why is that?"

"Just means you're gonna give the business to somebody else at the other end."

"But what if you don't know where you're going?"

"Oh, you know all right. People know. Or they could always change a ticket."

They could? "Did the other woman know where she was going from Hong Kong?"

"I didn't ask. There are people you don't ask. And she was one of 'em. You don't ask why, what, where or how. Said she wanted to go somewhere and disappear. So I get out my cruise brochures, tour books, the whole enchilada—"

"You mean she came in here not even knowing where she wanted to go?"

Sammy gave me a confidential squint. "I get plenty o' odd balls in here, you know. And I get to figuring people out real fast. That lady knew she wanted to go to Hong Kong, all right."

"Why didn't she just say so?"

"Who the hell knows?" Sammy squinted again. "Never looked me straight in the eye."

I was careful to keep my gaze steady.

"Maneuverin' me, that's what she was doing. Shovin' me around on some invisible chessboard." Sammy's black olive eyes studied my eelskin bag. "I had her figured as a shopaholic, too. Money. She reeked money. The rings. The car. White Mercedes. A real beaut. She had it parked right out front, in the No Parking zone. Watched the cop write out a ticket. Didn't bother her one damned bit. Paid cash for the airfare, too." Sammy drew a fresh chestful of Salem. "So when do *you* want to leave?"

"Friday."

"October ten?" Sammy turned to his computer. "We'll see."

I watched his long dirty fingernails click away on the keys. Then his face contorted to read the information blipping up on his screen.

"You want a stopover?" he asked. "Honolulu, Seoul, Tok—"

"No. I just want to get there."

Sammy slumped over on his monitor. "Oh, Jesus, Mary and Joseph, that's what she said!"

"Oh?"

"Yeah." Sammy resumed his sporadic dialog with the computer. "You got a preference for an airline?"

"Which one did she take?"

"China Air. Refuels in Taipei. Nice service."

I brushed a billow of smoke out of my eyes. "Fine."

"First class?" His tone was hopeful.

"Did the other woman?"

"Nope. Savin' her money for some big shopping spree, I spose."

"Why don't I do the same?"

Sammy snorted disapproval. "Flight 005, departing LAX three-fifteen Friday afternoon, October ten. Arrive Hong Kong October twelve. You gotta cross the International Dateline, you know."

"Yes, I know."

"Non-smoking?"

I nodded.

"Window seat?"

I nodded again.

"I figured." His fingernails clicked away on the keys. "Okay. You're on board. Now, what about a hotel reservation?"

"Did she?"

"Yeah. Just for one night, though. Crazy. There's no money in a one-night hotel reservation. Doesn't even pay me to do it."

"Where?"

"Where else? The Peninsula." Sammy fortified himself with another handful of Raisinettes. "My idea, not hers. Far as I'm concerned, the Pen is *the* place in Hong Kong. Always has been, always will be."

I smiled naively. "I'd like one night there also."

"What is this anyway?" Sammy shook a fresh Salem out of a near-empty pack. "After that, then what?"

"I don't know. I really don't."

"Okay, okay. I'll do it for you this time," he grumbled. "A single?" Sammy glanced at me. "Yeah, she booked a single, too."

I nodded as he French-inhaled his Salem and popped another handful of Raisinettes into his waiting mouth.

O

From Tripout Travel I headed for Mandeville Canyon and an appointment with Silvia and Elena. Silvia had phoned to ask me to consider taking her case. I told her I was leaving for Hong Kong and would have to put it on hold for the moment, but that I would like to review the scene of the crime once again. I wanted to fix it in my mind, so that my subconscious could play around with it on my journey towards Sally Barrett.

As I approached their front door, I heard music. Violin and piano. Vivace. Vivaldi? I waited for a pause between movements before I rang the bell.

Silvia and Elena were both in jeans and long-sleeved blue blouses, rolled up above the elbow. They greeted me with warm handshakes and sad but hopeful smiles. I told them I didn't want to interrupt their rehearsal, and that I'd simply appreciate having a few minutes alone in the patio. By the time I was standing on the rear steps once again, they had launched into another movement. Adagio. Exquisite. And so incongruous with the ugly image I was forming of Manuel's final struggle. Here, beneath my feet.

Questions were racing through my mind as I walked down the steps. If the burglary was indeed faked, why would the murderer wait until the end of Manuel's three-week visit, just two days before he was scheduled to leave for Madrid? And what murderer are we talking about? According to Silvia, her father had come for a rest, and only family intimates knew where he was.

I crossed the yard to the shrine, wondering if Manuel was perhaps trying to escape out the back door when his assailant caught up with him. I picked up the foot-high Madonna. It must have weighed ten pounds. Why would the murderer have left the house to get it? Or had Manuel run out the back door, grabbed it, and was heading back inside to clobber the intruder?

I was replacing the Madonna in her niche when faint scraping sounds came from the other side of the wall. It was Thursday morning. Wasn't Bill at work? Had Sally perhaps returned? I placed one foot gingerly on the side of the shrine, grasped the top of the wall with my hands and pulled myself up a few inches to peer over. The pool man was hauling his vacuum hose across the slate decking. I ducked before he caught sight of me. A gut reaction left over from childhood, I suppose, from my years of spying on the neighbors. Even back then my curiosity had flared out of control, and my amused—and often embarassed—parents used to call me The Little Spy.

I waited until Silvia and Elena had finished their adagio to take my leave. I told them that Dick would be getting in touch with them, and that as soon as I found Sally, I'd give their case my full attention. With that, I walked out to my car.

Next door, the pool man was loading equipment into the back of his pickup truck. He couldn't have been more than thirty, and had a lean, hard-belly look. Sandy hair, pulled into a little ponytail at the neck. A hip stubble of reddish beard. Snow-white T-shirt and jeans. He moved with a nice animal grace and looked to me like he'd sit a horse well. He belonged in a Dick Francis novel.

"Hello," I said. "I'm Paige Taylor. Are you Randall Waite?"

"Randy will do."

"I'm the woman who phoned you the other day regarding Sally Barrett's disappearance."

"Right." He tossed an empty chlorine container into the bed of the pickup.

"You said you didn't see much of her."

"Right."

"You're giving me the impression you didn't like her."

"Right."

"Or me either."

"Sorry. But I've got a string of pools to do this morning."

He reached into the cab of the truck and punched a button on the radio. Country Western music came on strong.

I said, "I won't keep you."

"That Sally Barrett cost me time. All the other pools I do around here on Wednesdays and Saturdays. But no. She's gotta have me come Mondays and Thursdays. What the hell's the difference to her? Couldn't she jockey a couple o' days around?"

"Bill—"

"The Doc's okay. Too bad he hooked on to that one. So she split, huh? Well, here's hoping she doesn't come back."

Randy Waite bolted into the cab of his pickup, threw it into gear, made a U-turn and shot out of Crestview Lane.

I bet that more than one woman on his route didn't care what day he did her pool. Bet he got a few offers from the guys, too.

O

With my eyes wide open, I spun the globe in my library and deliberately stopped it with a finger on Hong Kong. This is too easy, I was thinking, when the phone rang.

"Dick here."

"Dick where?"

"Would you believe Cicero, Illinois?"

"I would."

"And can you guess what I found in Cicero—also known as Little Poland?"

"A nest of Romanskis."

"Including Sally's parents."

"Bravo!"

"They're alive and well and working in a Jewel grocery store. He's a butcher and she's a check-out clerk."

I stretched out on the couch. "I'll bet you gave them one of your ring-a-ding stories and charmed them into conversation."

"And into taking me home with them to dinner!"

"I'm impressed!"

"Seamy side of Cicero. Near Cermak Road. Little house by the elevated station that they've been living in and paying for since the day one. But immaculate inside. Crocheted doilies on armchairs—"

"Silk flowers—"

"You've been there!" Dick chuckled. "Anyway, I stay for beer and brats. Mr. Romanski's homemade Polish sausage."

"Ummmm."

"And they tell me that's where Leona and her five brothers were born. They do not refer to her as Sally, by the way, nor did they even know she is a.k.a. Mrs. William Barrett."

"Five brothers?"

"All living in the area, too. But Sally was the star of the Romanski show all through her early years. The brains, the prize beauty. Anyway, the family thought that their little Leona was going to make a perfect schoolteacher, marry a local boy, have a nice big Polish family and all. But she had it bad for the stage."

"I'm sure you can identify with that."

"So she goes to Paris for her junior year, comes back the following fall 'in a family way,' as Mrs. Romanski puts it. Has an abortion and drops out of college."

"And out of the family."

"They want nothing to do with her. And I do mean *nothing*!"

"Did they know the gentleman in question?"

"No. Just that he was French. Story goes that when Sally was a student at the Sorbonne five years ago, she rented a room from his mother. But the Romanskis don't want to hear about either of them ever again. They have no idea where she went or what she did after that. And they don't want to know."

"No old letters she would have written them from Paris?"

"Nothing. Zero. They packed up what belongings she left and either gave them away or threw them away."

"I'm curious to know what brand of stardust you sprinkled in their eyes...."

"Let me save that for later. I happen to be at a sleazy pay phone by the El station with two tough-looking dudes across the street casing me. Besides, I'm so full of beer I could burst." Dick cleared his throat. "I'd like to proceed to the Loop now and the shelter of the Palmer House.

"And a loo."

"I'm desperate!" Dick blew a mouthful of air into my ear. "Nearly out of control."

"Just one last item. I'm leaving for Hong Kong Friday."

"Hong Kong!" Dick yelled. "Not going to Paris with Pat? She knows?"

"Not yet. But I think I just heard the front door."

"Gird your loins," Dick said, sounding oddly like Peter Lorre. "So what's the scoop?"

"U-Needa-Cab's Dick phoned me back last night. He remembered where he left Mrs. Barrett at LAX."

"And the winner is?"

"China Air. That led me to Sally's ticket and from there to her travel agent today."

"Fantastic!"

"Also discovered that she cashed out her checking account. But I'll save the details for when I see you at LAX Friday afternoon. We'll have a good hour to swap stories before I take off."

"We will?"

"So what are your two thugs doing?"

Dick paused. "Guess they split."

"Don't take it personally, Ace. *Ciao.*"

I replaced the phone on my desk and listened to what I suspected was Pat rattling about the kitchen. Next, footsteps approached my library door. It opened slowly, nudged by a bare toe. Pat appeared in a gold muumuu all aflutter with birds of paradise. She was carrying a silver tray decorated with a bottle of champagne, two Baccarat flutes, crackers, lemon wedges, cream cheese and caviar.

"Coffee, tea or Mumm's?" she murmured.

I said, "Mumm's the word."

She gave me a wink and curled five bare toes in my direction. "A little something to get the evening off on the right foot."

"Pat...I...I have something to tell you...."

"I'll just bet you do."

Pat put the tray down on my desk, hiked up her voluminous skirts, stepped over my legs and straddled my lap. With her nose nuzzling mine she said, "I suppose Billy Barrett has convinced you of the joys of multiple sex partners?"

"No," I said. "Give me monogamy."

"Here."

Before I could say 'Hong Kong' there was a tongue playing with my right ear, making rational thought, much less speech, impossible. It was long past dinnertime before I got around to mentioning that little British colony in Asia.

Chapter Six

Pat and I had half an hour en route to LAX to stop by Grimm and Barrett. It was Bill's idea, and I thought it would be a good chance for Pat to meet the rest of the cast.

We arrived at noon and Alyce Maine ushered us into Bill's office. There we were soon joined by Freddie and GG. Bill walked in a moment later.

"Couldn't let you take off without wishing you *bon voyage*," he said. "If," he added, turning to Pat, "that's how you pronounce it."

"That will do nicely," Pat said aloud. But the look in her eyes said, "No, that is *not* how I pronounce it." Like most francophiles, Pat cringes to hear French mispronounced. A reflex we barbarians have to forgive them.

But Bill didn't pick up. "I suppose you were born in France?" he queried, adrift again in Pat's emerald eyes.

"No. Boston."

"Go to college there, too?"

"No. Brown."

Time to change the subject, I thought, and I asked Bill where he bought his Krugerrands. "I want Dick to find out where Sally unloaded them," I explained.

Bill exchanged guilty looks with the Grimms before he finally mumbled, "Tijuana."

"No declaration of purchase," I surmised aloud.

"I think you'd better convince Freddie here to get his in a safe place," Bill said. "Not that GG is going to run off with them—"

Freddie laughed nervously and GG looked embarrassed. I was incredulous. "Don't tell me you've done the same thing Bill and Sally did?" The Grimms nodded sheepishly. "And in a 'safe' place in your home?" They nodded again.

I moved next to Freddie. I said, "Sally's influence?"

"'Nothing's good as gold,' she used to say," he answered. "She had a fistful of reasons why Krugerrands were the only safe investment there is. And, of course, the smartest. Nobody knows who owns what. No names. No paper trail. No tax."

"An easy way to launder money," I noted. "And Hong Kong is just the place—"

"For a Chinese laundry," murmured Pat.

"According to Sal it's not really income tax evasion either," Freddie continued to Pat. "Just a 'tax avoidance scheme,' as she puts it. Buy them offshore and sell them offshore. Meaning outside the U.S., of course. The only country where it's illegal not to declare purchase and sale." Freddie turned to GG. "We've already decided to do something about our stash. Diversify our savings." GG nodded. "I've contacted an investment counselor, and as soon as I can make up my mind how much to put where, I'll get rid of the Krugerrands. We'll have to declare them, I guess. Either that, or it's back to Tijuana."

"Or directly to jail," said Pat, *sotto voce*, "without passing Go or collecting your two hundred dollars."

"One thing Sally couldn't convince us to do, though," Freddie said, "was sell our house." He glanced at his office partner. "God knows she tried! But we kept it. Nothing posh, but we paid off the mortgage a few months ago. Free and clear." He wrapped an arm around GG. "Smooth sailing from here on in!"

The office door opened and Alyce Maine came in bearing a tray of finger food. Also a manilla envelope. From this she pulled a memo pad and desk calendar and handed them to me.

"I don't know if it's important," she said, "but Lieutenant Bashore stopped by the office this morning. He returned a couple of things that Carole Oliver had on her desk. Said you had talked with him yesterday on the phone and might want to see them."

The pad had office notes that looked like they came from telephone calls. Dates, names, numbers. Supply lists. I flipped the calendar to August. There were two words written in the box for the day Carole died.

"Get keys," I read aloud.

Bill stared at me the way he did when I asked him for the keys to Sally's desk. A Uri Geller special. The kind that can bend a spoon.

"Keys," I repeated. "What's going on here?" I delivered my "I haven't much time" like an ultimatum.

Bill managed to clear his throat and said, "Carole had spent the afternoon at the gym, so she was working late. That's what her message machine said when I phoned that evening from JFK to ask her to pick me up at LAX in the morning. That was after I got no answer from Sal. So I called Carole at the office."

"The keys, Bill."

"I suppose she meant my extra set. Like I told you, I lost my keys somewhere between my hotel and the airport. I asked Carole to pick up my spare set, so I could get my car at LAX."

"Where was that set?"

"At the house. Just inside the pool equipment gate. I told Carole that Sal wasn't home, but if she stood on tiptoe she could just reach over the gate and grab them."

"You told this to Lieutenant Bashore?"

Bill shook his head. "I didn't want to get any more involved than I already was. You know, with the Mandariaga thing and all. Besides, Carole never did pick them up. I had to call Sal to come and get me that morning. I forgot to ask her to bring along the extra keys. When we got home, there they were though, right where they belonged."

Behind my back Pat mumbled something that sounded like: "He's short on genes, long on chromosomes." I love it when she speaks in tongues.

○

The waitress in the airport lounge took our order for three glasses of iced tea, and I settled into a corner table, flanked by Pat and Dick.

"So how did you appease the savage beast?" he asked.

"I simply took her to her favorite sushi bar," I answered. "The maguro and uni did the rest."

"You lie," said Pat.

Dick opened his briefcase and took out a thick paperback. "I saw this in O'Hare airport and read the jacket blurb. Lots of action in Hong Kong." He handed me *The Bourne Supremacy*.

"Robert Ludlum? Why, thank you!"

"Starts in a Kowloon cabaret." Dick grimaced. "In a pool of blood."

Pat gave my right forearm something between a squeeze and a pinch. "Reason enough to stay out of bars," she said.

"And French restaurants" flew out of my mouth, as if I was speaking in tongues. And for a moment a pair of ice-blue eyes was all I could see. They belonged to the Greek phenomenon. Melina.

Dick said, "By the way, Sally's parents did remember that she did a couple of Ibsen plays in college. Made a hit in *Hedda Gabler*." Dick sighed. "*Hedda Gabler*. Now there's one I'd *really* like to do! And that reminds me—did you listen to my phone messages for me?"

I nodded.

"The school called."

I nodded again.

"I didn't get the part."

"Sorry."

Dick twitched his mustache and sniffed. "They probably wanted a younger man."

"I'm afraid so."

"Something better will come along," Pat offered consolingly.

"Sure. Like what? Nagg in *Endgame?*"

The waitress set three glasses on the table and said, "Y'all enjoy!"

We did.

"By the way," Dick went on, "our Mrs. Barrett was not known as Sally or Leona Romanski in college. She took a stage name."

"The one she used for the post office box?" I guessed.

Dick nodded. "Lee Roman."

"Hmmm," hummed Pat. "Sounds like a *roman à clef.*"

"It may well be," I said. "I found out that Sally took the box in late October of last year. Just before Halloween—and her marriage to Bill. And she canceled it on September 16."

Dick slammed his fist on the table. "Ten days before she threw her scene and left!"

"Exactly. Also, remember Sally as a one-day brunette in May? Mulling that over prompted me to check with the passport agency. I found out that she had declared her passport lost and applied for another."

"Another Lee Roman?" asked Pat.

I said, "Sorry. Just Sally Barrett."

"But why the change to brunette?" Dick wondered. "And why two passports, assuming she didn't really lose the first one?"

"Well, if she *is* using the new one now and wearing her hair differently, it'll be far more difficult to follow her. With a little extra make-up, Sally may not be recognizable from the snapshots Bill gave me."

"If she didn't care about her past surfacing, she apparently does care about her future," Dick thought aloud.

"I don't buy any of it," Pat said flatly. "Sally wanted to be followed."

Dick sighed. "It looks as though she had been planning to take Bill to the cleaners for a long time."

"Sounds like you're both beginning to feel sorry for him." Pat leaned back in her chair. "Not I. Bill Barrett is a predator. Definitely one of the Lower Vertebrates."

A voice over the loudspeaker announced final boarding call for China Airlines' Flight 005 to Hong Kong.

Pat laid her cheek briefly against mine. "Be careful," she murmured. "I don't want a Paige missing."

O

After dinner I leaned back in my window seat, not in the mood to focus on the in-flight film or *The Bourne Supremacy*. As I always do, when I first set out on a case, I was entering a delicious period of limbo: a time when I step from the known into the unknown; when I say farewell to security, to habit, to love and hello to chance encounters—to what Pat would call the aleatory, the random. As she once said, when you travel abroad, all you have to do is walk out of your hotel room and adventure happens. Then she added that if you live around Los Angeles, all you have to do is stay home and leave your door unlocked.

I slipped on my sleeping mask, propped my pillow against the window, and leaned my head on it. I hoped I wouldn't forget where I was and inadvertantly wrap my arms around my silent seat companion. He was all lap computer and data sheets and looked to me like he needed a fix of Kaopectate.

I soon fell asleep. Sometime during the long night a vivid dream image began to form on my inner screen. Stretched across a spacious backyard were a dozen clotheslines, and pinned to them were towel-sized thousand-dollar bills, drying in a gentle breeze.

O

Eighteen hours later the 747 touched down on a runway at Kai Tak airport. A few minutes later, shouldering my purse and garment bag, I was off the plane.

I moved quickly through customs, out the door and down the ramp that led into the greeting area. It was a muggy October evening in Hong Kong. Probably just like the one that greeted Sally Barrett exactly two weeks ago.

Chapter Seven

I smiled into the froggy eyes of the reception clerk at the Peninsula Hotel. His lapel pin read MR. PENG.

"Do you have a reservation, Madam?" he asked.

"Yes." I handed him my voucher from Tripout Travel. "Would it be possible to have the same room my sister had when she was here in September? I believe Sally wrote that it had a harbor view."

"Her name is Taylor also?"

"No. Barrett. She arrived September 28."

The clerk turned to his computer with a polished efficiency. "Yes, Madam." He seemed pleased. "Mrs. Barrett occupied room number eight sixty-six, with harbor view. You are in luck. A gentleman checked out of it late this afternoon."

"May I trouble you to ask how long my sister stayed?"

"No trouble at all." Mr. Peng punched a series of keys on the computer. "She left us on...October 6."

"Six days ago," I mused. "Do you remember her by chance?"

"The name is familiar, yes, Madam."

"I have some photos of her with me." I spread them out on the counter.

Mr. Peng examined the pictures carefully, hesitated, then said, "I believe I do recognize her."

"You see, I thought I'd surprise her with a visit, but I don't know where she went from here. And I certainly doubt that she would have changed hotels if she had intended to stay in Hong Kong." I gave him a complimentary smile. "Perhaps she made some phone calls from her room? Asked for assistance in some matter?"

"I'll check her record for you." He turned to his computer again, studied the screen of his monitor. "Sorry, Madam," he concluded. "No record of any phone call. And Mrs. Barrett paid her bill in cash."

I collected the photos. "Sal always did hate credit cards," I sighed.

Mr. Peng took a key from the rack and handed it to a bellhop. "He will show you to your room, Mrs. Taylor. Please enjoy your stay with us."

○

Minutes later I stood by the window of Room eight sixty-six, eight stories above the tip of Kowloon Peninsula, overlooking Victoria Harbour. It was still as I remembered from a dozen years before—knobby with freighters, tugs, junks, sampans, sailboats and ferryboats. But not Hong Kong Island, with its new clusters of skyscrapers near the water's edge. Tonight they twinkled with a million lights.

"Wan Chai," I said aloud, fixing on the district directly across the bay. "Sailors' heaven." I wondered if Sally Barrett ever got to Wan Chai. Sally and Susie Wong....

I showered, pulled on my white robe and stretched out on the queen-size bed. I tucked my hands behind my neck and let my eyes wander lazily about the room. From the thick powder-blue carpet to the salmon drapes and matching bedspread, to the cream and gold French Provincial furniture. It was what I always like to do on a case. Put myself as literally as possible into the other's thoughts, feelings, footsteps. Until pursuer and pursued become as one.

Woman and sleep were about to become as one when the phone rang.

Mr. Peng said, "A call for you from a Gertrude Stein, Madam. May I put her through?"

"By all means."

The next thing I heard was Pat's "Hello?"

"What took you so long, Gert?"

Pat said, "Thought I'd give you time to shower. Have a good flight?"

"Super."

"Besides missing you *à la folie*, I wanted you to know that Dick and I stopped by Barrett's on our way home from the airport yesterday. Dick wanted to see where Bill keeps the spare keys. Like he said, right inside the gate. No trick to reach over and grab them off the hook. But Carole never did, apparently."

"And besides missing *you* like crazy," I said, "I've been thinking about Carole's planned itinerary. It makes no sense to me. From the office in the Palisades, down to Redondo Beach—sailing right by LAX—have a swim, zoom back up to Mandeville Canyon for the keys, then back down to LAX."

"Unless she forgot about the keys when she left the office," Pat suggested. "And then she died before she had to double back."

"Possible."

"According to Bill, when he phoned Sally that morning, she said she got home from the cinema close to midnight and hadn't seen or heard from Carole."

"But what if Carole did go straight to Mandeville Canyon from the office," I said. "Let's suppose Sally was actually home and told Carole that she would collect Bill. Maybe there was a jealousy factor. Maybe a quarrel."

"Bill swears that Sally suspected nothing between him and Carole at that point. He did admit that Carole would like to have replaced Sally as the new Mrs. Barrett. But, like Bill says, Sally was the—"

"Primary person," I yawned.

"I heard that. Time to kiss and say goodnight? Or would you rather dance?"

"Kiss-kiss," I said. "And let's dance."

○

Early the following morning I phoned room service and ordered a pot of espresso, then lay back on my pillow. What schemes must have been swirling through Sally Barrett's mind as she lay here? I wondered. And why here? Why eight days in Hong Kong? Was she simply trying to make up her mind where to go next? "I doubt it," I told the knock at the door.

The espresso arrived with a fortune cookie. I opened it and read: "Your fortune is as sweet as a cookie." Yo.

I poured myself a cup of coffee, drank it black, and ate the fortune cookie. Then I reached for the map I'd left on the nightstand. With my first finger on the dot that was Hong Kong, I imagined the possible directions of Sally's departure. The Philippines? Japan? That would be going backwards. How about India then? Or on to Europe? And what about mainland China?

I opened the telephone directory and began calling every airline that had operated a flight out of Kai Tak on October 6. But I struck out. No one had any record of any Barrett. Perhaps Sally really did mean to disappear from the ends of the earth, leaving no footprints.

I poured the last of the espresso and opened the telephone directory again—this time for C.I.T.S., China International Travel Service. I discovered an office in Tsim Sha Tsui, Kowloon's main commercial district, a block from the Peninsula Hotel.

O

A half hour later I was walking up Nathan Road. It was a banquet of smells, sights, sounds and rhythms. I relished it all. The traffic flowed British-style on the left, beneath layers of signs in Chinese. It was like an animated kaleidoscope that offered instant shifts in perspective—that special ingredient that adds spice to a journey.

I turned the corner at Peking Road. From there it was only a few steps to the entrance of C.I.T.S., and a short flight of stairs up to the office. Four Chinese clerks—two women and two men—were seated at desks with their clients. Most of them looked and sounded like Americans. I took a number and sat down to wait.

"Going into China?" The tenor voice next to me was filtered through a thick black beard and moustache.

I nodded.

"Me too," the voice continued.

"What a coincidence." I stifled a yawn and was glad when a clerk beckoned me to a desk.

"May I help you?" the young woman asked politely.

"I hope so," I replied. "I'm trying to locate my sister. She left Hong Kong on October 6 and went into China. I very much need to find her. A family matter. Could you tell me if she applied for a visa here? Her name is Sally Barrett. Sally Romanski Barrett."

"That name does ring a bell, as you Americans say. I may have helped her myself."

I took the photos of Sally out of my purse and spread them on the desk. "Perhaps you'll recognize her?"

"I'm not sure." The clerk shook her head. "But let me check our files."

"Thank you," I said aloud. And to myself, "I know. We Caucasians all look alike, don't we?"

The young woman disappeared into the rear of the office and returned moments later with a memo in her hand.

"Yes," she said, "Sally Barrett. Issued a visa on October 4. She also bought a train ticket for Guangchou for October 6 and booked a single room for one night in the Liu Hua Hotel."

"And from there on?"

"I have no idea. When you travel on an individual basis in China, you can book here only as far as your first destination."

"And then?"

"You make your continued travel and hotel arrangements as you go. With C.I.T.S., or train or bus stations, or C.A.A.C.—China Airlines—if you wish to continue by air. It's up to you." She took a sheet of paper from a drawer and handed it to me. "You are free to go to any of these cities."

"I didn't realize it was so easy these days to travel independently in China." I glanced at the dozens of open cities listed on the paper. "My sister isn't going to be easy to find."

"Maybe impossible." The clerk shrugged. "Do you wish to apply for a visa anyway?"

"Yes. How long will it take?"

"You could have it the day after tomorrow. First thing in the morning."

"I'd appreciate that. And I'd like a train ticket to Guangchou and a reservation for one night at the Liu Hua if possible."

"Certainly."

O

It was late afternoon when I returned to the Pen. In the lobby tea time was in full swing. A waiter in a crisp white dinner jacket and black bow tie and trousers seated me at a table and took my order for tea and ginger cakes.

Around me, tables were filled with Japanese business-men, assorted European couples, mix-and-match American tourists, even a few China dolls. I pictured Sally Barrett sitting across the room. Alone.

Alone? Perhaps Sammy Bandini was right—Sally's choice of Hong Kong really was premeditated. Maybe she had been conning Bill all along. What if she staged the entire relationship? Led a double life? Maybe the house seemed so impersonal because she had stored her possessions elsewhere. Did she know someone in Hong Kong? Was that the reason for the fifty-cent stamp and the post office box? But then, why did she book a single room in Guangchou?

The waiter returned with my order and poured me a cup of tea. His Mona Lisa smile told me he knew all there was to know about women traveling alone. I returned it with my Tiananmin Square special.

While the tea cooled a bit, I tasted a ginger cake. And winced. Did I imagine it, or did I really feel a twinge of a toothache? I found myself admitting that I probably should have had Bill check that tooth.

The amber sounds of two violins, viola and cello tuning to a piano's A drifted down from the balcony overlooking the lobby. The cushioned strains of *Anima e cuore* followed. Instantly, I was sitting with my parents in St. Mark's Square in Venice, listening to the orchestra, feeding the pigeons, asking for a sip of Campari and soda. Before the song had ended, years had passed. Two glasses on the table now sparkled with Asti Spumante, and passion was in the air like a wall of raging wind. A hurricane affair that would end here. In Hong Kong.

I sipped my tea slowly. Sally must have had a rocking love affair, too. With the father of the baby she never had. That year she was studying in Paris. Perhaps they too went to Venice. Perhaps they too heard *Anima e cuore* in St. Mark's Square.

I studied the tea leaves in the bottom of my cup. But all I could see was Melina. Love with the ice-blue eyes and the mahogany hair. The village of Stanley on Hong Kong Island. The French restaurant. The final scene. Yes, I decided as the orchestra began *Non dimenticar*, I would go there tomorrow.

Mr. Peng, now listing slightly to starboard, approached my table.

"Pardon me for disturbing you, Madam," he began, "but I happen to have a ticket for the Sing Ping Cantonese Opera this evening." He produced an envelope from his pocket. "Unfortunately, I will be unable to attend. We have a large group arriving unexpectedly, you see. But perhaps you might enjoy it?"

"How kind of you!" I took the envelope he offered, thanked him, and went up to my room to change.

O

An usher showed me to an aisle seat near the stage in the main section of the theater. I sat down, wondering if Sally Barrett had come here too. Wouldn't any opera lover?

The curtain lifted, and the stage filled with glittering costumes and the vibrations of another world. A language of raw shape, light, movement, color, sound and gesture. Just the thing to inspire Pat to write another erudite paper with some teasing title like: "A Semiotic Approach to Cantonese Opera and the Absurdist Paradigm."

My gaze drifted across the aisle to my right, to a middle-aged Chinese gentleman in a gray business suit. His head was ovoid and bald, with a drawstring mouth. And thin, dark eyes that seemed to look out of the face like a knight peering out through his visor. I had heard him humming and chuckling to himself hour after hour. And now, as the opera reached its climax, he turned up his own volume. The absurdist's dream, I thought. The spontaneous audience. Part of the perform-ance. Performance....

When it had ended and the house lights were turned on, I found myself exiting through the lobby door next to him. He was still humming loudly and laughed as he caught my eye.

His "You liked?" was pure staccato.

"I loved it!" was my legato reply.

We went down the steps of the theater together.

"You go to *Star Ferry*?" he asked.

"Yes."

"We go together."

"I'd like that."

"I am Mr. Yum."

"I am Paige Taylor."

"I was opera singer," Mr. Yum announced. "I was Prince Dik in *Unfinished Romance in Phoenix Chamber*. You know?"

"Yes," I replied, remembering my program notes. "A hopelessly complicated plot, I'm afraid," I added, hoping he wouldn't quiz me on the details.

"Not complicated. No. Very simple." Mr. Yum was ada-mant. "Ngai San-tin mistaken after pirate attack for pregnant Princess Hung-luen who in love with Kwan-hung. San-tin rescued by Kwan-hung, who must marry missing Hung-luen, and taken to Prince Dik. Hung-luen saved by father of San-tin, Ngai Si-on, but she have lost memory. Due to concussion, remember?"

I nodded invisibly.

"And Si-on give her to San-tin's fiancé, Sheung Chuen-hau," he went on. "But Kwan-hung see Hung-luen at house of Sheung. Hung-luen disguise as man to go to house of

Prince Dik, who give her San-tin for bride. And San-tin also pregnant, and both true and false princess give birth to child on their wedding night!" Mr. Yum laughed uproariously.

"How simple can a plot be?" I murmured.

"Cigarette?" Mr. Yum offered me an odd-looking pack.

"No, thank you."

"You not smoke?"

"No."

"Too bad," he smiled, lighting his own. "Cigarette is sign of civilization."

Mr. Yum inhaled deeply, blew the smoke vigorously into the air and began to sing. As we walked through the streets towards the *Star Ferry* pier, I found myself humming along.

On board the ferryboat that crossed from Hong Kong Island to Kowloon, harbor lights twinkled in the background as the *Unfinished Romance* underwent its second performance of the evening. But this time it was sung half in Chinese and half in an unintelligible tongue, with me as the maiden Hung-luen.

"We drink now?" was Mr. Yum's suggestion as the passengers prepared to disembark and scatter into Tsim Sha Tsui.

"Why not?"

I followed him down Salisbury Road and into a quarter filled with tailor shops, boutiques, camera and jewelry stores and strip joints. Mr. Yum stopped abruptly in front of one particularly sleazy establishment.

"Look!" His drawstring mouth pulled up into a half-moon as he pointed to a large color photo of a naked couple caught in the act. His eyes looked like slits in a cement bunker. "You like?"

"Like what?" I asked quietly.

"We go in." He reached for my arm.

"You go in," I said, maneuvering out of range.

"*We* go in."

"*You* go in. I go on."

I slipped between two grinning streetwalkers, darted down the crowded sidewalk and into a labyrinthine arcade of shops and passageways. In moments Mr. Yum was nowhere in sight. I soon emerged on Nathan Road and headed towards the Peninsula Hotel. I was humming softly to myself and musing on the plot reversals in the *Unfinished Romance*— with Carole Oliver on my mind.

Chapter Eight

A swashbuckling dream about a pirate ship with a Captain Yum and a crew of two naked women was beginning to recede from my consciousness like an ebbing tide. Gradually I became aware of a telephone ringing.

I fumbled for the receiver and managed a husky hello.

An inflammable voice said, "You must have had quite a night!"

"I must have." I read my watch. "Almost one in the afternoon? Have I overslept!"

"What about last night?" Pat wanted to know. "I phoned my fingers to the bone. Chilly and rainy here and no one to light my fire."

"I unexpectedly went to the Cantonese Opera. Met a Mr. Yum, whom I later eluded near a tacky topless and bottomless bar in Kowloon. Be glad that I didn't wind up in Ricky and Pinky's Tattoo Parlour in Wan Chai, with a red rose on my—" I adjusted a pillow behind my head.

"On your what?"

"My *what*, by the way, is leaving tomorrow for the Chinese mainland. By train to Guangchou, old Canton. Picking up Sally's trail was almost too easy. She's dropping croutons, not crumbs."

"Well, here's another one for you from Dick. He's at an audition, but asked me to tell you that the Grimms are in a dither over dumping their Krugerrands. Apparently they've opted for a trip to the Cayman Islands."

"By chartered plane, I assume. When are they leaving?"

"End of the month."

"Well, we all know what the entertainment's like in the Cayman Islands."

"Beach to beach banks?"

"Whose lips are sealed. Little old Georgetown must have a couple of hundred of them. And most of them private."

"Our Dick also said to mention that he isn't getting anywhere with coin dealers. But he did make contact with Silvia Mandariaga, and they drew up a temporary contract."

"Pat, ask Dick to get in touch with Bill's gardener, will you? I think Bill said that he works for Silvia as well. See if he remembers any changes in either yard after Manuel's death."

"Like signs of a struggle?"

"Who knows?" I said. "By the way, what's Dick's audition for today?"

"Sounds like some state-of-the-art porno flick," Pat giggled. "*Top Bun.*"

I pulled a pillow over my face and groaned.

Pat asked, "So what's next on your agenda?"

"Breakfast in bed, I suppose."

"Ummmm. Sounds yummy."

"It could be," I said.

O

I finished my orange juice, *omelette fines herbes* and hot croissant and poured myself another cup of espresso from a white porcelain pot. Then I settled back into the soft padded chaise longue by the windows for some leisurely reading. That's something else I like to do on a case—give myself plenty of free time for my subconscious to play cat and mouse with a few chance ideas and let stray signs take on meaning.

First I unfolded the *South China Morning Star*, which had arrived with the breakfast tray. I scanned a few local news stories. Over-written. Sally Barrett's stormy style, too, I thought. She's probably the type that could stir up dust in a rain forest. Another Melina.

From the rack next to my chair I pulled out a magazine at random. *Discovery*. I flipped through it to an article entitled "Lobster Lust: Don Juans of the Deep." It told me that lobsters mate belly to belly. Ah, sweet mystery!

I poured myself a final cup of coffee. Replaced *Discovery* in the rack and picked out *Cruising World*. A personal ad at the end caught my eye. "Young semi-retired architect from Amsterdam," I read aloud, "looking for sharp, adventurous lady to share life eternal aboard luxury motorsailer currently berthed in Hong Kong. Signed, 'Searching.'"

"Good luck, Flying Dutchman!" I laughed as I replaced the magazine in the rack and got to my feet. "Sally Barrett, you may have missed the boat!"

I showered and put on a cool jade tank top and white cotton slacks and sandals, betting on heat and humidity. And as soon as the lobby doors closed behind me, the air was sticky and still. But I decided against a taxi and the tunnel to Hong Kong Island and headed instead for the pier. I would make the pilgrimage to Stanley today just as Melina and I did on that farewell trip. A pilgrimage, yes. To the shrine of first love.

Oh, I'd had a few other flings before Melina. I was twenty-three when we met, twenty-three when we parted. But it was with her that love first flared into grand passion. The forever syndrome. I thought we were going to be together for all eternity, Melina and I. Like Sally and her Frenchman, I suppose. Like all young lovers.

The *Star Ferry* took me across Victoria Harbour, and from there I walked the few minutes to Central Station. Then, in a front row seat on the upper level of a double-decker bus, I rode once again through Queen's Row East. Past imaginative skyscrapers with glassy penthouses that tower over street-level shops. Over cramped living quarters which tour guides call quaint.

Beyond the outskirts of the city, the bus careened over the curving strip of a road towards the far side of the island. Something in the feel of the hills, the glittering blue bay and the patches of sandy beaches in the distance still reminded me of Amalfi Drive. Amalfi, where it all began, and where it should have ended. With the ring. That 'gift from a relative.' Then the letter that was 'strange, when no one knows our address.' And the rendezvous in Venice that was 'just a trip to the post office.' Yes, Melina, I followed you. Found you. And Charles. And yes, I left you. Oh, such grand displays of passion you put on then! Flinging your ring into the Grand Canal! Swearing you would never see him again. Until your 'business trip to Hong Kong,' that is.

"Business trip," I muttered to no one in particular, as the bus pulled into the terminus at Stanley. I wandered down into the village. Roamed the familiar narrow passageways of the market. Tried going through the motions of pricing furs and silks. Useless. The empty beach was far more compelling.

The French restaurant there still had the same plain exterior. Inside, the same set of stairs. An open balcony above. Rattan tables and chairs. The same view out over the beach and the bay. And the sailboats and the mossy hills beyond were there just as they had been before. As if they would be there forever.

I settled into the corner table by the west wall. Might as well go the whole route.

"Red vermouth, please," I told the waiter. "Martini & Rossi, if you still have it. With a twist of lemon."

"*Oui, Madame.*"

I leaned my head against the back of the chair and watched the sunset trail rainbow ribbons across the bay. Watched it frame again those terrible ice-blue eyes and their jagged, double-edged life. Their brutal Mount of Olives mentality. Their denial. Their betrayal. Funny, how that old feeling materialized, too. Those four chambers of my heart squashed into one.

I could still see it: Charles' telegram, carelessly concealed. Typical, Melina. Typical. All part of your power trip—creating one-sided passions, and the scenes they thrive on. The scenes you lived on to divert the truth, to avoid the real you.

The waiter returned. He placed a glass of vermouth on the table and offered me a menu.

"Madame would like to order dinner?"

"Yes, she certainly would." Madame was, in fact, starving. "Do you still serve sweetbreads in mushroom sauce?"

"*Mais oui, Madame!*"

"*Salade de saison....* And may I have the wine list, please?"

"*Bien sûr!*"

The waiter headed for the bar, leaving me to wonder if Sally Barrett had a few things in common with Melina. I sipped my vermouth and remembered that honeysuckle hell I once called paradise—then paradise lost. What was there to lose but my nostalgia for a dream of my own creation? Like nostalgia for a childhood that never was. For all paradises that never were. I couldn't let go of Melina until I stopped believing in what we never had. It took me four years to get my priorities straight. It took meeting Pat.

So much for first love, I thought. The pilgrimage was over. The shrine empty.

It was time for a toast. I lifted my glass.

"To you, sweet love," I said, as the puzzled waiter handed me the wine list.

Chapter Nine

The following morning I stepped out of a taxi at Hung Hom, the Kowloon Railway Station, and followed the arrows on signs that read "Direct Train to Guangzhou." They ended at a gate and a long ragged line of waiting passengers. Mine was the only Caucasian face among them. Minutes later the gate was opened. I followed the line up two flights of stairs and out onto a train platform. I glanced at my ticket, then found car Number 38.

Inside, a center aisle separated rows of seats four abreast. Each one had a fresh white doily on the headrest. I spotted Number 13, next to a window. I stowed my garment bag in the luggage rack overhead and settled in.

I had the feeling that my quest for Sally had just begun. That this was the true jumping-off place, the initial stage of some mysterious rite of passage. And I was the initiate, about to see the unseen, to know the unknown. Or so I hoped.

A nearly toothless, wizened Chinese woman with bulging hand baggage wiggled into the seat next to me, chattering in Cantonese. I chattered back in English. We smiled at each other in what I was certain Pat would call a blissful combination of pre- and post-lingual non-communication.

The train lurched into motion promptly at ten forty-five. I spent the next few hours watching the New Territories of Hong Kong flash by. What will happen to it all in 1997, I wondered, when Hong Kong reverts to mainland China? What is China *really* like these days? All I could remember of it was my father carrying me on his shoulders along the

Great Wall. It was snowing, and my mother was throwing snowballs, and we were all three laughing.

From time to time the Chinese woman offered me food from her voluminous bags. Oranges, yogurt, bread. I bought us both cans of San Miguel beer from a bright young hostess pushing a cart of drinks and cigarettes up and down the aisle.

Then barbed-wire fences and watchtowers announced the border, and the People's Republic. After the customs officials had passed through, the Chinese woman headed for the lavatory. When she returned, I decided to follow suit.

Inside the tiny cubicle was an opening in the floor in the shape of a toilet bowl, with two small rectangular raised platforms on either side. The flush chain was bent and broken in half. "Fallen in the line of duty?" I asked the apparatus. I looked around further. No paper in sight. No surprise.

As I combed my hair in the dusky mirror, I recalled my teenage project to write a documentary book entitled *Round the World with Johns*. It was to describe everything from French *pissoirs* to Turkish toilets. From types that displayed utter simplicity to others that were insanely puzzling. Their shapes and background décor. The methods of flushing— push or pull, raise or lower, jerk or handle with care. And the varieties of paper, when provided. I remembered in particular the individual sheets that once graced British government offices in London. They were of the texture of waxed paper, and each one bore the proud seal of the crown of England.

I replaced my comb in my purse. Now then, I asked myself, what would Sally Barrett be daydreaming about in here? Golden Oscars? April in Paris? Certainly not French *pissoirs*! I folded my arms and stared beyond my own image in the mirror. "Would Sally even be here?" I wondered aloud.

At five after three, exactly on schedule, the train pulled into the noisy maze known as the Guangzhou Railway Station. I said goodby to my seatmate and stepped out into China.

It was hot, humid, gray, and starting to sprinkle. And there was no mistaking the pain inside my jaw now. It was definitely a toothache.

At an information counter I found that the personnel and I had no language in common and perhaps little else, either. They pointed me out of the station and around the corner to the C.I.T.S. office.

There, three young men speaking broken Berlitz seemed more than happy to accommodate me. I displayed my photos of Sally Barrett. These they obviously enjoyed. They even thought they recognized her. But I suspected that they were confusing the subject of the snapshots with actresses they had seen in Hollywood films. Their spokesman discovered, however, that a Mrs. Barrett had booked the Guilin Holiday Inn from their office for three nights, October 9, 10 and 11. If Sally left Guilin on the twelfth, I figured, I was only a few days behind her now.

"Is it possible to phone C.I.T.S. in Guilin to find out where she went from there?" I asked.

"Such information impossible. You go to Guilin."

"How far is it?"

"Not far," the spokesman replied.

"How do I get there?"

"You can go by train."

"Where do I get a ticket? From you?"

"No. Train station."

"This station?"

"No."

The three thumbed through a well-worn pocket dictionary and conferred in Chinese.

"East station," they finally announced.

"When does the train leave?"

There was a long pause.

"You go to train station."

"How long does it take?"

"What take?"

"To get to Guilin?"

The three conferred again in Chinese.

"Thirty-six hours."

"Let's talk airplanes," I said. "May I buy an airline ticket from you?"

"You go to C.A.A.C. office."

"Where is that, please?"

"There." The spokesman pointed out the window to a nearby building.

"Now may I reserve a hotel with you?" I asked.

"Your name, please?"

"Paige Taylor."

"Your profession?"

"Professor," I answered cautiously. "Professor of French."

"Ah, good!" All three young men seemed quite pleased.

"But I must tell you that Guilin Holiday Inn is full now," the spokesman added. "And first you must get plane ticket. There." He pointed out the window again.

Nearly two hours and four long lines later, I had an airline ticket for the following day for the one-hour flight to Guilin and a room reservation for two nights there. Then I took my life in my hands. Amidst a menacing cacophony of horns, I dodged taxis, trucks, pedicabs, and hordes of cyclists to cross the several lanes of the boulevard that separated the C.I.T.S. office from the Liu Hua Hotel. With every step I took, a single question revolved in my mind like a carousel with a lone figure perched on its platform: Why would a racy Sally Barrett plod through all this dull hassle just to see a corner of China?

I changed money in the hotel bank, checked in at the reception desk, and was led to my room by an impressively polite young man. No sooner had he left than there was a knock on the door. I opened it to a teenaged girl and a vacuum cleaner.

"I clean?" she asked, shyly.

I looked around the immaculate room. "If you like," I said, and headed downstairs to the coffee shop.

With the exception of the waitress and the menu, it looked surprisingly like a hotel coffee shop chain in the States. Something in me said no to marinated beef and greens and yes to steamed snake with Chinese herbs. I also ordered a glass of the only wine listed. A red wine which, I noted, cost one yuan. About twenty-five cents? In the rear vision of my mind, I could see Pat arching an eyebrow. No matter. I agree with the French: a dinner without wine is like a day without sunshine.

The waitress arrived with the wine, easily contained in an object that was something between a thimble and a shot glass. She stood on one foot and then another as I sipped the strange, sweet liquid. When I looked up and smiled and ordered another, the young woman was radiant. "Welcome...to...our...hotel," she said, and bolted towards the kitchen.

"Welcome to China," I said to myself.

Just after I had returned to my room, there was another shy knock on the door. There stood another bashful teenager, this one clutching a thermos and gesturing that she would like to exchange it for the one already on the table. Oh, pul-leez!

"Hot," the girl said. "Hotter more."

She not only exchanged thermoses but began to clean the table top. Twice. And then moved on to the dresser. I shrugged, picked up the telephone and asked for the international operator.

After I had placed my call, I had a sudden flashback to childhood and to my favorite playmate, a neighbor boy named

Jimmy. On rainy days we would take turns chosing an imaginary friend or relative in some exotic spot around the world. Then we'd pick up the phone and ask for directory assistance—which in those days was free—in whatever country we wanted to call. We loved talking with the operators, telling them our bogus tales, listening to the incredible variety of their accents.

I remembered names like Ali Kazan in Baghdad; my imaginary Uncle Maurice De Gaulle in Algiers; and the one connection that the operator actually put through to London, to one Elizabeth Jennings, which left me utterly speechless.

It was almost an hour later when I heard a familiar voice. "Pat?" I said.

"You expected to find Billy Barrett in our bedroom?"

"I can hardly hear you."

"Want to hang up and dial again?"

"No, no, please!" I answered quickly. "It took me all the calories from my snake dinner to make this connection."

Pat's faint voice asked, "You had steak for dinner?"

"I'm in Guangzhou," I said into the crackling static. "Going to Guilin tomorrow. Sally went to Guilin." There was a knock at the door. "Someone's knocking at my door again."

"This is awful!"

"They probably want to vacuum again."

"Want to what?"

"Come in! Yes, go right ahead."

"What's going on there? Paige, have you been drinking?"

"I have consumed four thimbles of wine."

"Thimple? What's that? Chinese for liter?"

"Yes, you may remove the cover, thank you."

"Remove the what?"

"Pat, I want to tell you about Stanley, sweetbreads—"

"Stanley who?"

"Oh, no! Not clean sheets, too!"

"Hallo?" interrupted a bass voice. "Ist dis rrroom ser-viss?"

Chapter Ten

The following morning a taxi deposited me near the departure area of Guangzhou Airport, and I joined the snaking line of passengers waiting to check in on China Airlines' nine-forty flight to Guilin. The garlic in the atmosphere was even denser than in the Rome subway at rush hour. I implemented an exercise that a holy man in Rishikesh had once taught me—either to still my thoughts or to avoid foul air—and began breathing minimally.

Just as I was about to check in, the clerk changed the time on the departure sign from nine-forty to one o'clock. He noted my expression, apologized for the change and handed me a food voucher. "You go to restaurant," he said. "Out door. Left."

His directions led me through a set of double doors with a sign that read FAST FOOD in English. Inside were dozens of large round communal tables. I sat down at the only empty one, virtually unnoticed by the other customers who were eating voraciously, their chopsticks clicking and quivering in perpetual motion, their food slopping generously onto the tablecloth. Fat flies circled in the air, as lethargic as the hands that occasionally brushed them away. I had to smile at the incongruity of *La Bamba* blaring over the sound system.

Not even the waitresses seemed to be aware of my presence, even after half an hour. I began to wonder if perhaps the holy man along the Ganges was right when he told me that breathing exercises can make you invisible.

The voucher did finally prove to be good for a plate of sweet and sour pork and a bowl of rice. But the bottle of Tsing

Tao beer was extra, and lukewarm. Did Sally Barrett have a meal here too? I wondered. FAST FOOD was hardly in the fast lane.

Back in the main terminal the milling crowd was almost all Chinese, mostly men, and most of them were either smoking or clearing their throats and spitting. In search of quiet I wandered up a stairway, down a corridor, and stopped at a door with another sign in English: FIRST CLASS LOUNGE. But did I have a first class ticket? It was written in Chinese, and I could decipher only the date and price. "Who cares?" I asked the ticket, and opened the door.

The room was lined with midnight-blue armchairs and sofas, all backed with dainty white doilies. With the exception of a young hostess in a crisp white blouse and navy skirt, it was empty of humanity, and odorless. I sat down and let the silence embrace my ears.

The young woman eyed me shyly from across the room. Then inched towards me as if she were walking on thin ice that was about to crack.

"Meh I... see yur teeket, plez?" she asked.

"Yes, of course." I held it out to her.

The young woman went over to a buffet and carefully wrote something in a ledger. When she returned with my ticket, she also had a handful of index cards and a can of lemon drink with a straw in it.

I thanked her for the refreshment, relieved that my ticket had passed Go.

"I learn English," she faltered. "With these I practice." She handed me the cards, each one with a sentence in both Chinese and English. "Do you speak with me?"

"Yes, certainly," I answered. I read the top one aloud: "What is your name?"

"Hani," the girl beamed. "Your name, please?"

"Paige."

"Oooooohh!"

"How old are you?"

"Eighteen. How old are you?"

"Thirty-five."

"Oooooohh!"

I flipped to another card. "Where do you live?"

"Guangzhou. Where do you live?"

"California."

"Oooooohh!"

A dozen cards later I took out my photos of Sally Barrett.

"You see her?" I pointed first to my own eyes, then to Sally.

"Very...pretty." Hani nodded vaguely. "Very pretty lady," she said proudly.

The loudspeaker garbled something in Chinese.

Hani stood abruptly. "You go now. Must go. Plane to Guilin."

"I am very happy to meet you," I said in the present tense, having noted that neither the past nor the future was in the cards.

"I also," Hani said. "I very...sad...you go now."

"I am very sad also." I took her hand. "Goodby. May we meet again one day."

I shouldered my garment bag and purse and walked down the hallway to the stairs. When I looked back Hani was standing forlornly in the doorway, one hand holding her flashcards, the other waving farewell.

There was still a lump in my throat as I stepped inside the C.A.A.C. 737. Cantonese Opera was blaring out over the P.A. system. The passengers—all Chinese—were squeezing up and down the single aisle, talking animatedly and exchanging seats with wild abandon.

I had just decided that they were playing some Oriental version of musical chairs when a vision of a laughing Mr. Yum flashed onto my inner screen. Clad as Prince Dik in a regal robe of purple and gold, he was fingering a wispy black goatee. Twin princesses in scarlet and ermine knelt before him. Why this recurring image, I wondered, as I settled into my window seat and fastened my seatbelt.

By the time the stewardess appeared to hand out cardboard boxes of orange drink, the entire atmosphere radiated garlic. It oozed from the walls, seemed to filter through the P.A. system and breathed through the overhead air vents. Minutes later the stewardess reappeared, now passing out small white plastic boxes. I opened mine. It contained a black bow tie. I was delighted. It was that touch of the totally unexpected that makes travel my passion. A passion Sally Barrett must share, I figured, if she bypassed comfortable organized tours to strike out into China on her own.

Tea was the final item to be circulated. I sipped mine and winced. Prayer time. Oh, please, Allah, Vishnu, Holy of Holies, Whoever, please don't make me see a dentist in China.

Then the wheels of the aircraft touched gently down on a runway at Guilin Airport. Soon I stood at the curb outside the entrance and hailed a taxi.

"Li River Hotel," I told the driver.

"Li Jiang." He opened the rear door of his vehicle.

"No. Li River."

"No. Li Jiang."

"Why not?" I stepped into the taxi.

O

"You are Professor Taylor?" The young man at the reception desk seemed overjoyed. "I am Mr. Fong. Michael is my Christian name."

"I'm happy to meet you." I reviewed his square cheeks, decorated with a stunning pair of dimples.

"I am the manager of the Li River Hotel."

I smiled. "Also known as Li Jiang, from which I deduce that jiang means river."

"You're right." He studied my face with an inscrutable intensity and said, "Your plane was late."

"Yes." I noted that the lobby was filled with Americans and Europeans and wondered briefly how and why he had singled me out to observe a detail like that.

He asked for my passport, took down the information on a card and asked me to sign it. "I'm going to give you a discount on the room rate. Not 130 but 120 yuan."

"That's very kind of you."

"I will show you to your room."

Mr. Fong took a bundle of letters from a drawer, locked it, pocketed the key, and mumbled something of a confidential nature to the receptionist. Then he came out into the lobby and shouldered my garment bag. What now, I wondered, as I followed him up a flight of stairs and down a corridor to Room 106.

Inside, arms folded, I stood by the desk and watched in silence as Michael Fong carefully hung my garment bag in the closet. Next, he made sure the air-conditioning was working properly. Then he closed the corridor door and approached me.

With a disarming smile he said, "I need you to do something for me."

"Oh?"

He stepped to my side.

○

"What a marvelous connection!" I exclaimed. "As if we were in the same room!"

"It's about time!"

"Hold on a second, Pat.... Thank you, Michael. See you later then?"

"Downstairs? In the bar?"

I nodded.

"Around seven?"

"Fine," I said, and he closed the door behind him.

"What's going on there now?" asked Pat.

"That was the hotel manager. He insisted on supervising this phone call. Actually, he was lying in wait for me at the reception desk when I arrived."

"So your reputation preceded you to Guilin?"

"He was looking for a professor."

"About half the student body at UCLA is, too. Some even have a real fetish about it."

"He's twenty-one years old, very intense, rather brilliant, I would guess, and quite attractive."

"You think bisexuals, like blondes, really have more fun?"

I laughed. "He needed an American professor. Me, of course, simulating you. For obvious reasons."

"What did he say to me?" Pat wanted to know.

"That he was filling out forms for the University of Texas, Austin, and would you please look them over and see if he had done everything properly. Including a statement saying that he agreed to take their English prep course and will send them one hundred dollars."

"And then he hit me for the hundred?"

"Certainly not! Another letter in his bundle was from his 'rich uncle'—a Hong Kong shipowner who has assured the University of his support. To the tune of seventy thousand dollars."

"Some fortune cookie!"

"Any news there?"

"Guess who phoned me." Pat blew into the phone.

"Next time Dr. Barrett calls, tell him he can take part of his bill out in trade."

"I beg your pardon?"

"My toothache's getting worse." I put my hand on my cheek. "Tell Bill that hot tea hurts and cold beer feels divine."

"I'll let Dick deliver the messages, if you don't mind. And, speaking of our Dick, he is now trying to get the phone away from me. Hold on—"

"Hello, Boss. Just wanted you to know that yesterday Bill told me that the Grimms are supposed to leave for Grand Cayman on the twenty-fifth, if that's of any interest. Apparently Freddie's a nervous wreck. Missing work because of the shakes."

"I can see why."

"I'm getting nowhere trying to find Sally's address prior to the studio apartment she was living in for those few months between the time she first met the Grimms and moved in with Bill. The building manager said he saw almost nothing of her. Other tenants said much the same."

"Sounds like just another base camp."

"But I found the coin dealer on Wilshire Boulevard who bought the Krugerrands from Sally—about four hundred throusand dollars worth on the morning of September 26."

"Same morning as her scene in Barrett's office and her stop at Tripout Travel."

"Tight timing," was Dick's comment.

"Well-planned, too. Probably well in advance. But didn't Bill say he had closer to half a million stashed in the safe?"

"That's what he still says."

"So Sally might have cashed in the rest even sooner," I thought aloud. "Tijuana maybe? Where it wouldn't be reported. When she didn't want it known."

"But on the twenty-sixth she obviously didn't care any more."

"You know, Dick, I've been wondering if Carole did go to Bill's house? What if Sally discovered Bill's affair and had a motive for murder? Carole could have died there; in the pool."

"And then somehow Sally got her down to Redondo Beach," Dick added. "But she'd need help. At least a second person to drive Carole's car. With the body in one of the trunks."

"How about working on Lieutenant Bashore to check out the trunk of Carole's car as well as Sally's Mercedes. A chemical analysis of the interior of the trunks could prove interesting."

Dick sighed. "Wish *I* could get some interesting chemistry going."

I ignored that one. In the background I could hear Pat's "Oh, please."

"Now for the big news." Dick gave me his well-rehearsed breathless pause. "I got hold of Bill's gardener who also works for Silvia Mandariaga. He's from the Phillipines. They call him Phil."

"No."

"No speak English and my Tagalog's rusty, but I got his cousin in on an interview, and you betcha! Phil did notice changes in the landscape about a month ago. Some broken branches, a few flowers crushed, earth churned up. In the corner of Silvia's yard near the shrine. And in Bill's yard right on the other side."

I remembered my glimpse of Randy Waite in the same spot. "Like something or someone going over the fence."

"Phil hadn't heard anything about any murder. Reads the Manila papers, period." Dick rattled what was probably a page from his Steno pad. "Oh, before I forget, Freddie Grimm does remember Sally talking about Tibet. Like she'd really like to see the Potala Palace some day. Does that make sense?"

"It certainly does. If Sally had in mind to go there from Hong Kong, she would very likely enter from Chengdu—the capitol of Sichuan, north of here. And Guilin would be a logical stepping stone in that direction. I'll check out the airlines tomorrow." I paused. "By the way, how's *Top Bun* going?"

"I walked out the second day."

"Should I ask why?"

Dick cleared his throat before he said, "I'll give you back to Pat. I have an appointment."

I heard the phone changing hands and Dick and Pat exchanging goodbys. Then Pat's voice said, "Me again. I'm now lying on the hearth rug, in the glow of a booming fire."

"In your zebra lounging pajamas?" I wondered.

Pat gave me a spicy, "Vaiting for you to haf your vay vis me."

That brought to mind one sultry Sunday morning last summer, and left me speechless.

Pat went on to tell me what happened with *Top Bun*. "Apparently the director tried to put the make on our Dick over dinner in her pad. He fled."

"Who is she?"

"Ora somebody."

"*Ora Pro Nobis?*"

Pat giggled. "Now and forever!"

O

Early the next morning Michael Fong and I were standing on the rooftop of the Li Jiang Hotel. "Over there." Michael pointed into the distance. "That's the Holiday Inn. And down there is Shanhu Lake. See the bridges?"

I nodded.

"Ronghu Lake over there, and that is called Elephant Trunk Hill."

"Only because it looks like an elephant drinking in the river."

"Yes!" Michael laughed. "And what do you think of our beautiful mountain peaks? Thumb-shaped, would you say?"

"Just the kind you see on Chinese scrolls, oddly enough," I smiled.

"Now tomorrow we will go bike riding," Michael went on. "And on Sunday I'll be free all day and I'll take you on a riverboat down to Yangshuo. You'll see the limestone cliffs, the little villages, the bamboo groves, the caves—"

"Michael, that sounds wonderful, but first let me see what happens today."

"Perhaps I can be of some service to help you find your friend."

"You already have."

I left the hotel a few minutes later and followed Ronghu Road towards the Holiday Inn. The air was exhilaratingly fresh, unlike the mugginess of Hong Kong and Guangzhou. The chain of lakes, the bridges, the canals, and the streams of bicycles all reminded me of Amsterdam. But the beer can in the gutter read Tsing Tao, not Amstel, and most of the cyclists were wearing basic blue.

Through the doors of the Inn I entered another world. A space of sparkling chandeliers, huge brass floor-to-ceiling pillars, and rust and black marble floors, perpetually polished by two inconspicuous young women pushing soft mops. Beyond the wall-to-wall window a patio glittered with fountains and blue umbrellas cocked over white tables, radiant in the morning sunlight.

In the lobby a dozen Japanese businessmen relaxed on leather chairs and sofas, all looking well-off and pleased with themselves. Now this, I almost said aloud, is Sally Barrett territory. Jet-set prosperity. The Krugerrand Club.

The friendly desk clerk seemed to recognize the woman in the photos I showed him. He also told me exactly what I needed to know. Sally Barrett arrived on October 9, purchased a ticket for a riverboat cruise on the tenth and checked out on the twelfth. The records showed, too, that she had the hotel help her with a reservation in Kunming, for the three nights of the twelfth through fourteenth. That meant that if I could get to Kunming today, the seventeenth, I'd be only two days behind Sally. Otherwise the gap would be dangerously widening.

I walked briskly back along the lakeside to the center of Guilin. Knowing now what to expect, I stormed the C.A.A.C. booking office on Zhongshan Road like Jeanne d'Arc heading at full tilt for the British.

The throng inside was particularly frantic. Elbows jabbed ribs, feet crunched feet, and bodies pressed hotly together. Mindless atavistic reactions of the lower layers of the human brain, I thought, programed to fear being left behind on some perilous migration of the species.

Wreathed in the ubiquitous odors of garlic and tobacco smoke, I struggled to deactivate my olfactory lobes. When I finally reached the ticket window, I took up as much space as I could, spreading my arms out on either side and gripping the counter. Either occupy the entire space, I had learned, or be replaced or out-shouted. But the occupation was in vain. A clerk assured me that there was no seat available to Kunming for five days.

I directed my leaden feet back to the Li Jiang Hotel. Michael saw me enter the lobby and hurried over to me.

"What's the matter?"

"A toothache, I'm afraid."

"Do you need a dentist?"

I shuddered. "That will have to wait, thanks."

"What about your Sally Barrett?"

"She went on to Kunming, but I had no success getting an airline ticket. I suppose I'll have to take the train. How long does it take?"

"Too long. But can't you stay the weekend?"

"I'm afraid not, Michael, much as I would love to. If I get any farther behind Sally, I could lose her trail."

"Then give me your passport," he told me firmly. "And two hundred yuan. Foreign Exchange Currency, of course. About fifty dollars U.S. I have a friend at C.A.A.C. He owes me one."

I did as I was told.

"Now go up to the restaurant, order lunch, and I'll find you as soon as I can."

I went.

I had just finished a plate of fried rice that was pink and yellow with shrimp and eggs when Michael appeared in the doorway. His expression was a dead-ringer for Michaelangelo's reclining God on the ceiling of the Sistine Chapel, nonchalantly calling Adam into life by the mere touch of His finger.

Michael handed me a C.A.A.C. ticket along with my passport. "Tomorrow's flight," he announced. "Leaves at two-twenty, arrives in Kunming about an hour later. Do I make you happy?"

"How can I thank you?"

"Go bike riding with me," he answered. "Unless you'd rather see a dentist."

"Take me to your bicycle."

○

I pedaled the strawberry ten-speed behind Michael Fong along the quay by the riverside. It was a sunny, breezy autumn afternoon. Water buffaloes were tethered along the shoreline, grazing among ducks, chickens, geese, and an occasional swan. Women waded in the shallows, scrubbing laundry, draping the clothes to dry over the cement railings along the walkway, next to quilts and blankets out for an airing. Sampans, crawling with children, were anchored not far from shore. Here and there flat-topped barges awaited tourists for a cruise.

At the bird market we stopped to chat with the parakeets, poke among the bamboo cages, examine the ceramic pots for sale for feather-food and drink. I exchanged stares with a puffy, intimidating owl wearing a jeweled collar and leash.

"Bet you're not for sale," I told it.

We pushed our bicycles on through the dog market. Past a silky shepherd standing patiently near her owner, her soulful pup beside her in a wicker cage. I slipped my hand through the bars to scratch the puppy's ears, wanting to take him home with me. I shudder when I think about the canine connection in Chinese cuisine.

Is this what Sally Barrett came to China for? I couldn't help but wonder as Michael and I turned our backs to the quay and cut across a busy intersection. Would this have been her kind of afternoon?

No. I answered my own question as we pedaled back towards the hotel. The Holiday Inn maybe, and the riverboat trip. But not all the in-betweens. "Something's askew here," I murmured, as we dipped into the hotel driveway. "Out of focus."

"What did you say?" Michael asked.

"Talking to myself again," I answered. "But by the way, Michael," I added, "UT at Austin is going to love you!"

Chapter Eleven

I smiled when the stewardess handed me a white rectangular plastic box. Another black bow tie inside suggested that the airline's seemingly random events were becoming predictable. I wondered if Sally Barrett's trail would soon do the same.

Two hours later a dilapidated airport bus carried me, together with a few dozen Chinese and a Danish couple with backpacks, to an obscure parking lot in Kunming. The Chinese scattered immediately, while the Danes studied a map in Nordic silence. I walked out to the street, opted for the nearest corner and a right turn. Luckily, the first block produced not only the C.A.A.C. office but, adjacent to it, the Kunming Hotel.

After checking in and inquiring about Sally Barrett, I followed the receptionist's directions into a room next to the hotel lobby. A little man was seated there behind a large, barren metal desk. His eyes spelled cocky.

"I would like to telephone this number in California, please," I said.

"You must give me one hundred yuan," he told me, "and I will give you change when you finish. You wait here," he added, coming out from behind the desk and pointing to a bench. "When connection is made, you get phone in booth number three."

I handed him a banknote and watched him strut back to his desk. His two-inch wedge heels thrust him so far forward that his knees seemed about to buckle. I wanted to tell him that tall is no more beautiful than small.

A half-hour later the phone rang in booth number three. I stepped in. It stank of cigarette smoke from its previous occupant.

"Pat?" I asked. "Can you hear me?"

"Yes. But you sound like a loudspeaker at a French train station. Noisy and garbled."

"I'll make it short then. I'm at the Kunming Hotel."

"Where?"

"In Kunming."

"Nothing in this world is more dazzling than binary logic."

"It may well be the only logical element of this trip thus far. The receptionist here just told me that Sally Barrett left Kunming October 15, three days ago. Headed north for Chengdu. I'm booked on tomorrow's flight. Still hoping to close the space-time gap between us before she disappears into Tibet. That appears to be her trajectory."

"You haven't heard the latest," groaned Pat. "Are you sitting down?"

I looked down at the floor of the phone booth, half ashtray and half spittoon. "No, and I don't intend to," I said.

"Hold on a minute. Dick wants to tell you."

"Hi, Boss. Listen, I have tragic news," he began in his Day-of-Doom voice. "Freddie decided to avoid the expensive chartered plane caper and cash out the Krugerrands in Tijuana instead. The master plan was: one, sell them for cash; two, convert that into a cashier's check; three, fly commercial to Cayman; four—"

"Open his own private bank and set up a bogus company," I surmised aloud. "And five, draw the money out as he pleased by loaning it to himself. Also known as back-to-back borrowing."

"Exactly. But things didn't turn out that way. Freddie got waylaid."

"What?"

"In San Ysidro. The police found his Lincoln less than a mile from the border fence. Blood on the driver's seat. And a fresh Mexican cigarette butt in the ashtray, and Freddie doesn't smoke. The detective on the case thinks that whoever did it was riding with him. Maybe got in the car with him when he left U.S. immigration."

"Maybe with a gun in his ribs."

"Apparently Freddie had the cash with him, since the two briefcases GG said he had put the Krugerrands in were in the trunk of his car. Empty."

I blew a wheeuuu into the receiver.

"Police suspect that he was drug dealing. Their guess is that whoever iced him dumped his body in the ocean. The tide was going out, so he probably rode out with it."

"Poor Freddie! And he thought it was going to be smooth sailing from here on in."

"They're still searching for the body."

"How's GG?"

"Catatonic. But at least she's in no financial trouble. The house was paid for, and Freddie had a fat insurance policy from Metropolitan Life."

"How's Bill taking all this?"

"Trying to be a big brother to GG. Working six days a week."

Baritone and mezzo mumbles preceded Pat's, "Yes, even *I* am beginning to feel sorry for Barrett. In spite of his *Quest for Fire* dialog."

"Bill's working Saturday," I thought aloud. "Freddie's day off. The day Sally didn't want Randall Waite to clean her pool." There was a brief pause before Pat and Dick gave me a chorus of: "Whooaaa!"

"Dick, find out the date on that insurance policy, will you?"

"Check."

"I'll phone tomorrow from—"

After an ear-shattering crash came silence. I walked over to the little man behind the desk. He shrugged nonchalantly and said, "Finished." And handed me thirty-eight yuan in change.

○

"I wash?" the chambermaid was asking me an hour later.

I handed her a pair of jeans and a denim shirt, and with my index finger made a mini-circle on my wristwatch. "You return at ten tomorrow morning?"

"Yes, yes."

Previous experience made me hold up ten fingers. "Sure?"

"Sure, sure."

I headed for the lobby and Dongfeng Boulevard. Knowing that Sally had booked no tours in Kunming, I had no fixed directions. And I hadn't much time.

I wove my way through throngs of pedestrians, probably just as Sally had done four days ago. I crossed side streets, dodging the steady streams of cyclists, motorcycles with sidecars, jeeps, trucks, vans, taxis and buses. Always alert for the sounds of Sally's footsteps. Watching for the footprints that were growing fresher every day.

Qingnian Road was a blue and olive smear of street hawkers,cubicled vendors, and hordes of shoppers. People cooked, ate, yelled, haggled, laughed, coughed, spat. A bicycle repairman was fixing flat tires on a gray patch of sidewalk. A shoe repairman was carving out a new sole while a customer waited with one bare foot. Ducks were hanging by their necks in an open market. Gaffed beef was dripping with blood and flecked with flies. From a music shop came *Canta y no llores* sung by Los Tres Ases. I stood still on the sidewalk and shook my head at the incongruity.

I started across an intersection and was nearly hit by a cycle-pulled cart drawing a tray of slaughtered pigs piled three feet high. It ran amuck at the next corner. One wheel was in the ditch when I arrived at the scene, and all the pigs at an incredible slant. Their unblinking eyes looked immensely puzzled. Mine, too, I suppose, as I imagined Sally Barrett here. The incongruous, I thought, *reductio ad absurdum*.

Qingnian Road led me to the gates of the Kunming Zoo. Inside, I watched a knot of people clapping their hands at the raw-bottomed monkeys. The clever inmates began to imitate their visitors. Suddenly a shiver ran down my spine. I felt like Sally was following me instead of me following Sally. On the murky fringes of my mind some idea was pulling into focus.

From the zoo, I walked on randomly through a series of narrow streets choked with exhaust fumes and the smoke of open cooking fires. The combined odor of garbage, grime and garlic followed me all the way to a lakeshore.

I circled the lake slowly. Its glaucous mossy water told me that limited perception is what hides the unknown and makes it appear nonexistent. And *that* is the author of all mystery.

"Ah, but how to open the doors of perception?" I asked aloud. "Before it's too late."

There was no answer.

O

Back in the hotel, I showered and went downstairs to the restaurant for dinner. I had just finished a plate of pea pods with mushrooms and laid my chopsticks aside when my young waiter again approached my table.

"Where you come from, Baby?" he asked politely.

"California," I answered, wondering who had had the fun of teaching him English. "And you?"

"Daquing."

"Where is that?"

"I show you."

He removed my empty plate, took a pencil out of his pocket, and drew a sketch of China on the paper tablecloth.

"You see?" he grinned. "China in shape of chicken. I born here. In chicken head."

I smiled. "You've come a long way, Baby!"

"Where you go from Kunming?"

"To chicken tail," I told him.

"You see Dragon Gate here?"

"No."

"Bamboo Temple?"

"No."

His black-olive eyes widened in astonishment. "What you see in Kunming?"

"The zoo."

"Zoo? You come from California to Kunming to see zoo?"

I shrugged. "Maybe."

He ambled away, shaking his head.

I paid my bill, went up to my room and switched on the television. A familiar face appeared. It belonged to Jodie Foster. Her mouth was not quite in sync with the dubbed dialog.

"That says it all, Jodie," I told the flickering screen. "This quest for Sally Barrett is not quite in sync with the real thing, either."

I went to bed, feeling like I was on a roll, but unable to figure out where the roll was going.

O

The chambermaid arrived at exactly ten the following morning with my jeans and shirt. They were perfectly clean, but too damp to wear.

Chapter Twelve

Flight 770 was five hours late, and it was close to midnight when I deplaned at Chengdu Airport. I now had a third black bow tie stowed in my purse.

Outside the baggage claim area it was misty and chilly. The air felt dank, on the edge of rain. I peered into the darkness and spotted a taxi. It was as dented and anonymous as Kinsey Milhone's original Volkswagen. I looked around for a driver. Suddenly a young man rushed to my side and nearly tore my garment bag from my shoulder.

"Taxi?" he asked. "I taxi."

"Good!"

"Jin Jiang Hotel?"

"Jin Jiang," I echoed, wondering if foreigners here ever went anywhere else.

I got into the rear seat of the vehicle only to find a woman already occupying half of it. The driver started off down a muddy road barely illuminated by dim yellow headlights. A pleasant voice next to my right ear said, "May I introduce myself? My Western name is Karen Chang."

"Paige Taylor." I took the woman's warm hand in the darkness. "You didn't arrive from Kunming?"

"Beijing. We landed only minutes before you. Just enough time to beat you to a taxi."

"I'm sorry. I didn't mean to force you into sharing it."

Karen Chang smiled. "My pleasure."

"Beijing is your home?"

"No. Chengdu. I'm returning from London, actually. A conference. I'll spare you the boring details."

"Not the kind during which you and your colleagues chloroform each other with papers?"

"I'm afraid so!" she laughed. "And my papers are in here." She tapped the briefcase on her lap. "I'll loan you one in case you have trouble getting to sleep tonight."

"Do I have a choice?"

"Would you prefer 'Flutter Analysis of Composite Structures' or 'A New Lanczos Algorithm for Eigenproblems?'"

I giggled. "Aeronautics?"

She nodded. "Research engineer."

"I adore titles," I said. "They're like mantras to me. They trigger altered states of consciousness if I'm not careful."

"Aummm," Karen began, in a voice an octave lower, imitating a monk chanting the sacred Buddhist word. "Aummmm. Aeroelastic constraintsssss... Interlaminar stressessss... Linear nonlinear equilibriummmmm...."

I laughed helplessly.

"Your turn now," she said. "Do you also write papers with koan-like titles?"

"No. Mysteries," I found myself freely admitting. "But once I find a title, the whole plot seems to spring into being. And now it's my turn to spare you the boring details."

"I doubt that they would put me to sleep."

"Don't count on it."

"Should I guess that your present protagonist finds herself or himself in Chengdu? And you've come to further the intrigue and dab in some local color?"

"I suppose I have."

"Are you divulging the title to a stranger in the night?"

I surprised myself with: "*Fool Me Once.*"

"May I look forward to reading it one day?"

"You may even find yourself in it."

"Distorted beyond all recognition, I hope!" she chuckled, as amber city lights began to line the road and asphalt replaced the mud. "Well, Paige Taylor, welcome to Chengdu!"

I could see her features now in the glow of the lamplight. She had soft black hair, almond-shaped eyes that radiated a catching *joie de vivre*, a full mouth and a smile that revealed a perfect set of white teeth. The kind, I thought fleetingly, that would put Bill Barrett out of business.

The driver said something to us in Chinese. I made out "Jin Jiang" but nothing else.

Karen answered him, then turned to me. "We are almost at your hotel."

"I hope the stop isn't out of the way for you."

"I live just down this street, actually." She pointed out the window. "But I'd rather spend a few more moments with you. I hope you don't mind."

"On the contrary."

"Since this is my city, I wonder if you'd be my guest and have dinner with me tomorrow? Who knows," she grinned, as the taxi pulled up in front of the Jin Jiang Hotel, "you may collect some new material for your novel."

"I'd like that."

Karen followed me out of the taxi. "Would it be convenient to meet at the hotel bar?" she asked. "Say around six?"

"I'll look forward to it." In the light of the hotel entrance I found myself facing a strikingly beautiful woman. She was perhaps a few inches shorter than I and a few years younger.

"Well, do be careful here," she cautioned with a wink. "You know what we say about ourselves: 'The Chinese have three hands. Two for their own pockets, one for yours.'"

"Thanks. I'll remember that."

A few minutes later I held a weighty room key in my hand. I entered the hotel elevator and pressed the button for the fourth floor. Suddenly the pain from toothache I had tried to ignore flared into the unbearable zone. I was overjoyed to find a mini-bar in my room and soon had a few ice cubes wrapped in a washcloth.

Cupping it to my cheek, I wandered out onto the balcony. The air was crisp and the streetlamps mellow and blurred in the thickening fog. Across the road and through the bushes there were soft lights flickering, and a faint music. I held my breath and listened carefully. A waltz. A Viennese waltz! If China was anything, I decided, it was inconsistency. So was Sally Barrett.

○

At eight-thirty in the morning I was buying a croissant at the pastry bar on the main floor of the hotel. In the nearby coffee shop I ordered orange juice and an espresso to go with it, then hurried on to reception. The clerk was accommodating. His records showed that Sally Barrett checked in on October 15 and out on the nineteenth. He also seemed to recognize her photos. Why shouldn't he, I thought, if Sally checked out only yesterday? I had no time to lose.

I located the C.I.T.S. office in the rear of the hotel. There had been flights to Beijing, Hong Kong, Kunming and Lhasa the day before, I was told, but for any more information I would have to contact C.A.A.C.

I took the elevator on up to the fifth floor and the Lhasa Hotel Service office.

"I wonder if you could tell me if my sister, Sally Barrett, made a hotel reservation with you a few days ago? She left for Tibet yestereday."

"Barrett? Moment, please." The woman opened a leger. "Yes. She reserved a single room at the Lhasa Guest House for three nights."

"Do you suppose I could phone C.I.T.S. in Lhasa to see if my sister has purchased an onward ticket from them?"

The young woman laughed. "Oh, no! Such things not possible."

"Can you tell me when the next flight leaves for Lhasa?"

"You must go to the C.A.A.C. office. Very near. Across the street from the hotel. Down Renmin Nanlu Boulevard."

"Thank you."

I dodged the bicycles in the lane next to the sidewalk, trucks, jeeps and taxis in the center lanes, another stream of bicycles, and finally set foot, intact, on the far sidewalk of Renmin Nanlu Boulevard.

Outside the C.A.A.C. office I studied a poster announcing Saturday service to Lhasa. Also continuing service from Lhasa to Kathmandu on Wednesdays. "Wednesday?" I asked the poster. "The day after tomorrow?"

In all probability, Sally was indeed booked on the Wednesday flight from Tibet down into Nepal. Her pattern thus far had been to reserve a certain number of nights and not extend her stay. And where else does one go from Lhasa? If only there were a direct flight tomorrow from Chengdu to Kathmandu, I could be greeting Sally Barrett in person before sunset on Wednesday!

I strode militantly inside and joined the line at the TICKET TO LHASA window.

Forty minutes later I was asking an agent if he could give me some information on a passenger going from Lhasa to Kathmandu.

"No information. Sorry. Next, please."

I held my ground. "Do you have a flight to Kathmandu today?"

"No flight to Kathmandu."

"Tomorrow?"

"No today. No tomorrow. No ever. You first go to Lhasa."

"Is there a flight to Lhasa—"

"No today. No tomorrow. Only Saturday."

"Next Saturday? The twenty-sixth?"

"Yes, but no seats."

"Is there a waiting list?"

"Yes. But too long. Too many people."

"When is the next flight?"

"Added flight on twenty-seventh."

"I'll take it."

Back at the hotel, I took the elevator up to the third floor office of China Travel Service. There I discovered that Sally had gone on an excursion to Emei.

I asked the clerk, "On what day?"

"The tour left on the seventeenth, returned on the eighteenth."

I got out my photos. "Do you recognize this woman?"

"Maybe, yes." He shook his head. "If hair was more dark. Darker more."

I thanked him and headed for the elevator.

My next words were directed into the receiver of my room telephone. "Dick," I said, "Did you get the date on the Grimm's insurance policy?"

"Would you believe last Halloween? Same day Bill and Sally were married?"

"Sounds like a double ceremony to me."

"Now hear this: our Pat came up with a brilliant idea—to check out the post office box again. Since Sally left no forwarding address, Pat thought maybe someone would remember either disposing of mail or returning it to senders. That burly guy finally told me Sally was getting a catalogue from West Marine Products. After she left, he started taking them home with him, he said. Thinking about buying a little sailboat himself."

"Tell Pat she has a major reward coming. I know she's up to her ears getting ready for Paris, but—"

"Dr. Towne told me to tell you that she's presently being fitted for a straitjacket."

"Give her my love," I said. Then suddenly a vision of Freddie in Speedo trunks flew by my eyes. "Mr. Kessler, how long will it take you to pack your razor and Lagerfeld and get to LAX?"

"I'm going somewhere?"

"Honolulu."

"Sand and surf? Mai Tais and mahi-mahi?"

"In Pernod sauce."

"I can leave tonight."

"I'm betting that Freddie was not buried at sea after all. That the murder scene was just as phony as Sally's hysterical farewell. What if he skipped town with the cash too?"

"And headed across the Pacific? And a rendezvous with her?"

"If Freddie did want to disappear with the loot and follow Sally, he would have cashed out the Krugerrands in Tijuana. Then left California with a cashier's check and little else. But first gone somewhere, en route, still in the U.S., where he wouldn't have had to give his real name and show his passport."

"Like to Honolulu as Fred Doe? Then, thinking no one would check out the Islands for a dead man, gone on to Hong Kong or wherever from there."

"Exactly."

"I'm on my way."

"And Dick," I added, "why not get your air ticket from Sammy at Tripout Travel? Make it a one-way, just in case. He'll love that."

"Am I missing something?"

"And treat yourself to the Hilton Waikiki."

A pleasant baritone rumble filled the receiver. "Must I?"
"You really must."

○

I sat at a table in the bar of the Jin Jiang Hotel, sipping a cool Manhattan and enjoying the magical effect it was having on my tooth. The assortment of hotel guests milling about was quite unlike the tourists I had seen before in China. Middle-aged couples outfitted in khaki pants and sweaters and heavy-duty hiking boots. Probably either going to or coming from Tibet. Snatches of conversation indicated several journalists as well, and at least a dozen college students in jeans and sweatshirts bearing names like Oxford and Princeton. Hardly Sally Barrett's set, I was thinking, when a gentle hand touched my shoulder from behind.

A voice said, "Hello."

"Hello." I tilted my head back and looked up into friendly almond eyes.

"No, please don't get up." Karen Chang took the hand I offered and sat down opposite me at the small table. Her trim beige business suit looked like London to me. She asked, "Have an exciting day?"

"I certainly did! After umpteen offices I saw the People's Park, the People's Stadium, visited the People's Exhibition Center, and went by the People's Swimming Pool. Riding everywhere, of course on the People's buses."

Karen laughed. "Heavy on the garlic, right?"

"But I enjoyed it all. I really did. I've fallen in love with your city."

"I'm glad. And now how about some People's food? Are you hungry?"

"Ravenous."

"I'd like to take you to Furong's for our special Sichuan Mapu Dofu, a rather spicy bean curd in minced meat sauce. Liberally rinsed down with Pijiu—People's beer," she added, with a wink. "The restaurant is rather tacky by American standards. It's not a tourist place. It's for locals and real travelers. I think you'll like it."

"I'm sure I will," I said. "But may I offer you a drink first?"

"Thank you, yes."

"What's your pleasure?" I signaled to the waiter.

"Whatever you're drinking."

I ordered two Manhattans.

Karen folded her hands and leaned across the table. "What on earth were you doing in all those offices today, if I'm not being too forward? Is there something I could help you with?"

I studied the invitation in her eyes for a moment, then told her the story of Sally Barrett's disappearance, my search for her, and the problem now of getting on to Lhasa. She listened intently.

When I had finished she said, "Sounds like the pieces of the puzzle are all there but just out of kilter. While you were talking I was reminded of the negative hypothesis theory. I often go that route when I get to a roadblock in my work."

"When a positive hypothesis gets you nowhere, but your subconscious is telling you you're on the right track?" I asked.

"Yes. So I start thinking in terms of proving the negative hypothesis false. Then it may become obvious that its opposite is true. In Sally Barrett's case, though, it seems somehow like you're inverting the strategy. Taking the false negative hypothesis as true to begin with, and that's why you're stuck." Karen sighed. "Guess I'm not making much sense."

"On the contrary. Please go on."

"If Sally didn't want to be followed, she's been very stupid about staging her disappearance, and she doesn't sound to me like a stupid woman. If she wanted to be followed, you're the donkey going for the carrot. But how long is that game going to go on? And then what?"

"You mean, as long as I play the donkey and there's a carrot in sight, all's well?"

Karen nodded. "But what if you don't? Paige, I think you should get some backup help. You may be in harm's way."

"It's too late to bring in help here."

"Then you'll have to have eyes in the back of your head."

"Funny you should say that," I said. "I keep having the feeling that in some way I'm being followed." I arched an eyebrow. "You're not working for Sally Barrett, are you?"

"You thought our meeting at the airport was coincidental?" Karen smiled. "I thought that rather clever."

I smiled back. "How about another Manhattan?"

Chapter Thirteen

I awoke with an excruciating toothache at three in the morning. Five sleepless hours later I went downstairs to the information desk and asked the clerk if he could recommend a dentist.

"Yes, of course," he answered. "One moment, please."

He opened the telephone directory, found a number, dialed, spoke briefly, and turned back to me.

"We are very close to the hospital, I am happy to tell you. Part of Sichuan Medical College. Do you have a map?"

"Yes." I pulled a map of Chengdu out of my purse.

"It is just here," the clerk explained. "Maybe ten minutes walking." He gestured towards the front door. "You will leave the hotel now, turn right, cross the river, and continue down Renmin Nanlu Boulevard. You can't miss it."

"I can't?"

"You will see the large red circle with a white cross in it. Go to Dentistry. They are expecting you."

"They are?"

"Just give them this." The clerk wrote something on a piece of paper.

When I thanked him, I realized that my speech had developed a peculiar lisp.

Ten minutes later a nurse was directing me to a bench in the hospital waiting room. The walls were off-white and scabby, the floor a mottled gray. I wanted to run.

A voice jerked me to attention. "Mrs. Taylor?"

I looked up to see a portly man with iron-gray hair and thick glasses walking towards me.

He said, "I am Dr. Leung, Chief Surgeon here. The Jin Jiang Hotel phoned and said you were on your way. Nice to be able to do an American a favor. I spent two years interning at Dakota Clinic. Fargo, North Dakota."

"I can't tell you how happy I am to meet you!"

"Will you come this way, please?"

I followed Dr. Leung down a dim hallway, up a flight of stairs and through a large room with three rows of eight dental chairs each—all of them occupied. A sight straight out of a Hitchcock horror flick. A smaller room adjoining it had only two chairs. One was vacant and the other contained an elderly man flashing what looked like a very rare and expensive mouthful of gold teeth. Before I knew it, I was sitting in the vacant chair with a cloth bib around my neck.

"Which tooth?" Dr. Leung asked.

I touched my sore molar with the tip of my index finger. "Hot hurts, cold feels good," I whined.

My new dentist put on a face mask. A no-nonsense assistant appeared, anonymous under another mask. Dr. Leung reached for a drill. "Open, please."

"What, no X-rays?" I asked.

Dr. Leung shook his head and turned on the drill.

"What?" I whispered. "No Novocaine?"

"Not necessary."

Bill Barrett's image appeared on my inner screen. He stood like Vandyke's portrait of Charles I of England. Hand on hip, he emanated unquestioned authority, the divine right of kings.

Ten minutes later the drilling had ceased, the pain was almost gone.

"Rinse?" The assistant offered me a chipped earthenware cup full of water.

I stared at the cup. "*Mashallah!*" I said, and rinsed.

"You need to see your dentist," was Dr. Leung's comment as he removed his face mask. "This is only temporary relief."

"I'll never forget your kindness," I told him.

And I never will.

Half an hour later I was back at the third floor China Tourist Office in the Jin Jang Hotel, twitching with excess adrenalin.

"Do you have an excursion going to Emei tomorrow?" I asked the manager, pleased to note that my voice was back to normal.

"Yes." He opened a notebook. "Oh, sorry. No, I doubt it. We need six people, and no one has signed up yet."

I gave him a wry grin. "What if I were to purchase six tickets?"

The manager stared at me. "We do not do that."

His tone was sobering. It told me not to waste his time asking why. "Are there regular buses going there?" I inquired instead.

"Yes."

"May I buy a ticket from you?"

"No. You go to bus station."

"Where is that?"

"Across river. And down." The manager gestured vaguely through the window behind his desk.

"May I reserve a room in Emei with you?"

"No. Rooms reserved only for tours. But not necessary. No problem in Emei. No tours going there now."

"What hotel do your tours go to?"

"Only one for foreign guests. Hongzhushan." He took a small map from a shelf of pamphlets. "This is Emei area, and this," he said, circling a name in Chinese, "means Hong-zhushan Hotel."

I thanked him and turned to leave, then noticed an announcement on the office bulletin board that read: "Foreigners are not allowed to entertain Chinese nationals in their hotel rooms. By so doing they may be apprehended by the police." I hurried to the elevator.

○

"Hello, Pat?"

"What are you doing in a rain barrel?"

"Wondering if you're all set to leave tomorrow evening."

"Air France. Nonstop to paradise." She paused, then added, "Alone."

"What are those munching sounds I hear?"

"Crackers and pâté. Mmmmm. Want a bite?"

"Umhum," I whispered.

Her "Here!" was followed by a tiny smacking sound, then: "So where are you? Still in Chengdu?"

"Yes. You can tell Bill Barrett that I've been to the most marvelous dentist here. I was charged two dollars and seventy-five cents to fill a cavity and eight cents for pain pills."

"At last—an excuse to phone him!"

"But right now I'm trying to get a flight out to Lhasa. Unfortunately, everything's booked until the twenty-seventh. Sally's trail leads into Tibet all right."

"Tibet, huh? Be sure to pick up some local color for me there." Pat paused. "Namely turquoise and coral...."

"Something that dangles?" I asked, thinking of the outrageous earrings Pat loves to wear. "Meanwhile, I'm going by bus to Emei for a few days. Sally took a short tour there. One of the four sacred mountains in China. Buddhist temples. Mist and serenity."

"Hoping to find some shred of a clue?"

"Maybe."

"Well, the latest here on our Grimm fairy tale is that they still haven't found a body. But then, it's a big ocean."

"The body may well be on the other side of it by now."

More munching preceded: "I thought I'd check up on Sally while I'm at the Sorbonne. They must have a record of her. An address. Might be interesting to speak with her former landlady."

"I was hoping you'd offer." I glanced at my watch. "And now," I said, "I've got to hurry out of this room. There's a woman coming here—"

"What's the matter? Isn't she housebroken?"

"She's a Chinese national who took me out to a Mapu Dofu dinner last night. And this afternoon she's taking me to the poet Du Fu's cottage."

"Mapudofudufu, what is all this?"

"By the way, my love, as soon as this case is settled, I'm going to spirit you away on vacation to the most romantic place on this good earth."

Pat asked, "Where?"

"I don't know yet," I said foolishly. "But I'll phone you at the Hotel des Marronniers as soon as I get back to Chengdu. How I wish I were going to be in Paris with you!"

"I may give you another chance."

I wished Pat bon voyage and a few moments later headed for the lobby. I stepped out of the elevator just as Karen Chang was about to step in. Apparently she wrote her own rules.

I took her hand. "Hello."

"How was your morning?"

I ran my tongue over my repaired tooth. "It's better now," I said. "And yours?"

"I've been having some fun with a pilotless airplane," Karen answered. "Looking for the optimal design, which may be just as elusive as your Sally Barrett."

We walked outside and Karen hailed a taxi. "What would you most like to see first?" she asked.

I said, "Why don't I leave that up to you?"

O

On the far side of the city our taxi skirted a long high cement wall before it pulled up by a gate. Karen gave some coins to an elderly woman at a nearby ticket window and led me into a complex of buildings and gardens, lotus ponds and stands of bamboo. It began to sprinkle, and we took shelter in a thatched-roof gazebo.

"This just happens to be where the great Tang poet Du Fu sat and wrote many of his poems," Karen said. "And your invisible woman has probably sat here, too."

"I think you come here often."

"I've even been known to recite the Master's poetry under this roof." Karen gave me a wink. "That is, when no one's around."

"No one's around now."

She began in Chinese, her tone gentle as the rain. "In English," she continued, "it goes something like this: 'In life we often drift apart, like stars that move in different skies. But what a night will be tonight, that we may share one candle-light.'"

"Your voice is as moving as the poem, Karen."

"And I just happen to know of a small outdoor restaurant that glows with People's candles. It's down by the riverside, across the road from your hotel. Will you have dinner with me there tonight?"

"Only if tonight is my treat."

"So be it."

On the way out we stopped in the main pavilion and Karen bought two slender matching volumes of poems.

She handed one to me. "Du Fu," she said, "in Chinese and English. Souvenir of Chengdu."

"And of a very special friend. Thank you."

Karen took my arm. "Now, will you risk a pedicab?" she asked. "I'm afraid it's nearly closing time and there may be no more taxis."

"I'd love it."

We walked outside the gate and climbed into an ancient rusty contraption. It was listing dangerously to starboard and reminded me of Mr. Peng at the Peninsula Hotel. Its proud owner was an old man, all sinew and bone sculpted in tattered gray pants and shirt. His bare feet hooked around the pedals like blackened parrot claws and set the vehicle in motion.

When the road led upward, we got out and helped pull. Downward, we clung desperately to the flimsy rail as the old man sat back, lifted his blue cap, and let his white whiskered head cool in the breeze. When it began to rain, we pulled the rotted cloth top over our heads and blinked at the raindrops leaking through the holes.

By the roadside life went on as usual. Inscrutable old men sat in bamboo chairs in tea houses. Barbers cut hair. Here and there BB guns were set up several paces away from boards with balloons. The sharp pops zapped Freddie back onto the target of my mind. Was I wrong about him? I wondered. Was he really gunned down after all?

We entered a narrow street of half-timbered buildings and the pedicab pulled to the curb. Karen announced, "Wenshu Monastery."

The curvacious hipped roofs of the temple were tile, the building itself black lacquered wood with a ruddy red and gold trim. Inside, worshippers knelt here and there on quilted prayer pillows. Giant black potbellied urns glowed with smoking sticks of incense. I gave a monk some coins, selected a stick, lighted it, placed it in an urn, and breathed its fragrance.

Karen said, "I'm sure you have the entire pantheon of deities working on the case now."

I smiled. "I was just asking them about your negative hypothesis."

○

In the open air by the riverside, Karen and I sat facing each other on wooden chairs at a rickety little candle-lit table. The dishes between us—which had been filled with rice, pork and mushrooms, and sweet and sour cabbage—were almost empty. So was a liter bottle of Tsing Tao beer.

I splashed the last of it into our glasses. "Here's to you and your pilotless plane!"

"And here's to solving your mystery." Karen raised her glass. "But be careful in Emei. They say many a pilgrim has leapt from the sacred mountain in sheer exhilaration!"

"Perhaps listening to the music of the spheres?"

"Perhaps. But still, I can't recommend it."

I cupped my hand to my ear. "Music. I hear that music from my balcony."

"There's an open-air dance floor next to the restaurant. Where the locals go to shuffle about. Would you like to—"

"Pick up more local color?"

"You must promise not to laugh."

○

The sign at the entrance to the dance compound read "NO FOREIGNERS ALLOWED" in English.

"So who reads English?" Karen asked. "Besides, you're not really a foreigner. You're one of us."

She spoke softly to the dim face in the ticket window.

I said, "I hope this little excursion doesn't get you into trouble."

"I never worry about such things."

I followed Karen inside—into another time zone. The records were Wayne King, from the forties as were the men's suits and the women's dresses. *How Deep is the Ocean* rolled out of the stereo speakers. I wondered briefly if Sally Barrett had done a turn or two on this dance floor.

○

"Why don't I lend you this so you don't freeze in Emei." Karen removed her brown suede jacket as we entered the lobby of the Jin Jiang Hotel. "It'll be chilly."

"But you—"

"I'll be going to Guilin on the twenty-fourth. Just for the day. Will you be back on the twenty-fifth?"

"Barring an irreversible religious experience, yes!"

"Will you have dinner with me that evening? And return my jacket, of course."

I laughed. "Karen, I've so enjoyed today. Thanks to you."

"You're a woman who would enjoy any day, thanks to no one."

We shook hands and exchanged goodnights. And as I turned to leave she said, "You remind me of another poem. 'Some day I must ascend the summit, and see how small other mountains are.'"

I could feel her eyes trailing me as I walked across the lobby and into the elevator.

Chapter Fourteen

"'How far would I travel...to be where you are?'" I crooned in the shower the following morning. "'How far is a journey...from here to a star?'" I turned off the water and reached for a towel. "How far indeed, Sally?" I asked the happy face in the bathroom mirror.

I finished dressing and had just zipped up my garment bag when the phone rang.

"Dick here," said a familiar voice. "Scenario: a room on the twenty-seventh floor of Tapa Tower at the Hilton Hawaiian Village, overlooking Diamond Head and endless scrumptious shoreline. Dick's powerful body is clad only in surfer shorts. His sexy feet are propped up on the balcony railing. His right hand is wrapped around an enormous Mai Tai whose rosy little umbrella he is about to remove to get his tongue on the goodies."

"Pineapple and such? Or is this an obscene phone call?"

"And cherry."

"I hate to rock your idyll with a banal question, but by chance has Freddie Grimm washed up on your beach?"

"Negative. But I do have news. I talked with Pat before she left for LAX. She said Lieutenant Bashore phoned. They found no trace of chlorine in either Sally's Mercedes or Carole Oliver's Toyota. As far as he's concerned, the case is closed."

"Sorry to hear that."

"But Pat had another tidbit for us. Said she phoned West Marine Products and found out that Sally had ordered a few things. Like heavy-duty sailing gear. The shipping clerk got a copy of the bill of lading. Mailed to a Marc Sancerre. General Delivery. Hong Kong Central."

"Dick, how long will it take you to pack?"

"I just got unpacked!"

"Position is not everything in life, as fools would have us believe."

Dick muttered, "Where am I going?"

"Anchorage."

"Alaska?" he bellowed.

"Honolulu will keep. Freddie Grimm may not. Alaska would be the second most logical place outside the continental U.S. for a change of name and plane, and a flight to Hong Kong. One more try. And try phoning me at the Jin Jiang day after tomorrow, in the evening—"

"Yeah, yeah, yeah. I know. Chinese date, Chinese time."

"From Anchorage," I told him, "with love."

O

I checked my garment bag with the fourth floor concierge. Carrying only my purse and a small canvas overnight bag, I took the elevator down to the lobby and followed the corridor to the telegraph office. There I wired two dozen red roses to Dr. Patricia Towne, Hotel des Marronniers, Rue Jacob, Paris 75006.

The clerk asked, "Would you like to enclose a card?"

"That won't be necessary," I answered. "I'll let the flowers speak for themselves."

Outside, it was chilly and grey. I was glad for Karen's jacket around my shoulders.

At the corner I bought three mandarin oranges and a bag of peanuts. My food and drink for the trip to Emei. Then I followed the riverbank footpath towards the bus station. Along the way I passed a group of old men hunched on chairs made of tree stumps. They were sucking on well-worn pipes and playing dominoes. One had built a miniature three-storey building with extra pieces. I watched as he gently touched it with a gnarled finger, and the entire structure collapsed. I moved on, but the domino effect lingered in my mind like an after-image in the eye.

Inside the bus station, controlled chaos reigned. People clutched plastic suitcases, bouquets of flowers and squawking chickens, while hawkers waved maps, sunglasses, soft drinks, shopping bags, bags of noodles and loaves of bread. I found an empty bench by the Emei bus stop and sat down to wait.

Opposite me sat a cheerful family of three: mother and father, both small and old before their time, and their sturdy teenage son. I wondered where they were going. On a long-dreamed-of holiday?

The woman opened a small plastic bag and drew out a pair of shiny beige socks. Husband and son smiled approval as she removed her shoes and took off a pair of well-darned anklets. These she placed in the plastic bag. Next, with her fingers, she carefully cleaned each space between her toes, then pulled on her new socks and held her feet straight out in my direction. Husband and son grinned and nodded. For this trio it was an event. And for me, humbling in its simplicity.

But so much for China on a shoestring, I thought. And so much for Sally Barrett. Certainly the joy of socks was not her bag.

○

The Emei bus looked as though it should have been sent to vehicle heaven directly following World War II. It had a reasonable horn for towns and an ear-splitting blast for the countryside. With its pointed front, it plowed through the muddy, potholed roads like the prow of a veteran tanker through the sea, scattering pedestrians, animals, cyclists and assorted trucks in its wake. Now, having picked up even more passengers along the way, it was stacked from front to back and floor to ceiling.

I sat next to a window near the driver. I was cold, even wrapped in Karen's jacket, and was glad for the body heat of the quiet man sitting next to me. From time to time I stole covert glances at his wispy Fu Manchu mustache while he appraised me with what looked like an orange-rimmed parrot eye. It had a glazed appearance and would dilate periodically, and I was never really certain what was appearing on its retina.

Endless chains of buildings huddled by the roadside. Some brick, some plaster, others half-timber. Some with thatched roofs, others with corrugated iron. All ant hills of humanity. In the rice paddies farmers working wooden plows and water buffaloes were knee-deep in chilly water and mud. Life in the slow lane.

In Meishan the man with the parrot eye got off. A young woman with a child strapped to her back took the seat next to me, tilting slightly forward to accommodate her cargo. I could barely make out a fuzzy head buried deep inside its blanket wrapping. In all the din and commotion, I thought, this silent baby must be an angel. Or dead. Or maybe both.

Life and death. Here they no longer seemed like irreconcilable enemies braced for an eternal struggle. Simply partners in a cosmic dance. A dance.... Strange, how Chengdu already seemed so far away, and plots of murder beyond belief.

Then the plains gave way to hilly country and terraces bushy with tea shrubs. Finally, in the distance, I could see mountains.

○

It was late afternoon when the bus jolted into a busy little town and a parking lot in between two nondescript buildings. All the passengers got off and the driver disappeared. I imagined that I must be in Emei.

A young man with a pedicab approached me.

I unfolded my map and pointed to the circled writing in Chinese. "Hongzhushan Hotel?"

He nodded vigorously and motioned for me to get in.

I crawled into the back of his cart for what I figured should be no more than a ten minute ride. I crouched down on the tiny board seat, bent over under the crumpled canvas roof. The young man hopped on the bicycle seat in front.

He peddled when he could and hauled the rig along when he couldn't. I held on to the side rails to keep my balance. I was frozen long before we had left the outskirts of town.

After nearly three quarters of an hour my cyclist coasted to a stop at a fork in a deserted road. He motioned for me to get out, gesturing that I should go on alone. His knees were shaking, and he was perspiring heavily. Why had he offered to do something that was obviously beyond him? Did he really even know where the hotel was? I crawled out and looked around. If nowhere is a place, I thought, this is it.

I gave the young man ten yuan and a look that was not the seal of Sino-American friendship.

Soon a handful of people began to appear along the road, then a string of shops. Was this another town or was this actually Emei? I showed my circled map to a man standing by the roadside. He gestured that I should continue.

I pointed to my watch and counted from one to ten on my fingers. "How many minutes?" I asked. "Five?" I held up five fingers. The man held up both hands twice. I thanked him and went on.

It was already seven o'clock and almost dark. The village was ending. In the distance the road snaked upward into the woods and the mountains. I shook my head. "A night in the forest?" I mumbled. "Fasting? Frozen?"

At the next fork in the road an old board was nailed to a tree. There was just enough light left to read "Hotel Hong-zhushan" and make out a faded arrow pointing left, up a short hill. Five minutes later I stood in the darkness before an unmarked building with a door that read "General Service Center." At the desk inside, a girl with a chirpy little voice told me that the restaurant across the street would be open for at least another hour, and that she had a room with bathroom for me.

"You must pay fifty-seven yuan now," she added. "About fifteen dollars American."

"It sounds heavenly." I handed her my passport and the money.

"Room four-one-two in Building Number Four." The girl pointed vaguely out the door and to the left. "Where Chiang Kai-shek and Madam Chiang once stayed."

Obviously, that fact was direction enough.

I went back out into the night. I stumbled along what seemed to be a path, then up a stone stairway towards lights flickering in the woods. Through a window in another building I saw a gray-haired woman washing dishes. I knocked and showed her the slip of paper the receptionist had given me. The woman dried her hands on her apron, picked up a thermos and a few packets of tea, and motioned for me to follow.

She led the way to a large frame structure enclosed in a wide wooden veranda. There she opened a door bearing neither a lock nor a number, flipped on a light switch and ushered me inside. She set the thermos and tea on a table, said something in Mandarin and left.

I looked around me. In a squeaky Chinese accent, I addressed the bare bulb dangling from the ceiling: "Wel-come...to...our...hotel!"

I was shivering, and there was no heater in sight. There was, however, what appeared to be a genuine bathroom, with sink, toilet and tub.

I put my sack of uneaten oranges and peanuts on the night stand near the bed. So Chiang Kai-shek slept here, I mused. What about Sally Barrett?

○

I was the last guest to enter the restaurant that evening. Most of the tables were already emptied of diners but still cluttered with half-eaten plates of food. There were enough leftovers on the tablecloths to feed at least a dozen more. As Karen had put it, this was the wastefulness of a people expecting to face starvation again tomorrow. They were playing royalty in the interim.

I sat down at one fairly cleared place and observed the giggling girls in white coats and trousers and black bow ties watching me from the kitchen doorway. Their leader, lithe and vibrant and with a cap of shining blue-black hair and starry dark eyes, came mincing towards me with a teasingly warm 'hello' on her lips. I told her she looked like a *Come to China* poster.

"I not understand," she said. "My name Ming. What you like?"

"I like to eat. Do you have a menu?"

"No. No menu. You get rice." Ming indicated an enormous battered tin basin on a table in the middle of the room. "I bring dinner."

By the time I had filled a dish with rice, Ming had returned to my table with a Paul Bunyan spoon and a bowl full of steaming surprise. This I tasted first, and deciphered a possible main ingredient of tripe floating in some greasy, fatty substance. Whatever this creature was, I thought to myself, it had definitely died in vain.

Suddenly an image of Pat appeared in the hollow of my spoon. She sat serenely in a restaurant in the Latin Quarter, savoring five-star *tripes à la mode de Caen*. I toyed with my own inedible enigma, trying to find a known among unknowns. Yes, I decided, this had to be added to my list of the ten most vile meals I had ever consumed.

Another one, oddly similar in texture and inscrutability, floated into my inner vision. It lay languidly on a tin plate in Afghanistan. I shuddered at the memory.

Ming minced back to the table. "You like?" she asked.

"It's most unusual," I answered. "Pijiu, please." I nodded towards an empty bottle of beer on an adjacent table.

Ming flew to the kitchen, returned with a bottle, filled a glass to the brim.

"You are English?" she asked.

"American."

"You like China?"

"Very much."

"Which building you stay?"

"Number Four."

The girl's eyes twinkled with some secret merriment. "I finish my work now," she burbled.

"Oh?" I asked quietly.

"I visit you tonight?"

"I'm afraid not." I flattened my hands against my cheek. "Sleepy."

"Maybe I visit you tomorrow?"

"Maybe," I said, wondering how I would get out of that one. I paid my check and lost no time finding my way back to the room. It was freezing. There was no hot water, and the toilet stubbornly refused to function. I went out into the woods. A three-quarter moon ducked in and out of the clouds, giving just enough light to see by. Not far from Building Number Four I came upon a Chinese gentleman standing next to a tree, obviously on a similar mission.

"More than one toilet *kaput*, I suppose," I said as I passed.

He answered in Chinese, laughing and gesturing towards the building with his free hand.

Back in the room I dove into bed under a mound of blankets and closed my eyes. Soon I was in Paris. And before I knew it, I was climbing up a tree in the patio of the Hotel des Marronniers. A chunky branch leaned towards Pat's room, the room we had shared there last year. My face was about to appear in her window with a "Surprise!" when a voice I couldn't recognize seemed to whisper in my ear. A woman's voice.

"What's a nice girl like you," it sniggered, "doing in a place like this?"

Yes, I wondered, as I drifted off into sleep, what *am* I doing here?

Chapter Fifteen

From my blanketed cocoon, I looked out the window. "I'll have eggs benedict and a pot of espresso, please," I told the thick fog that still clung to the pine trees and leaned heavily on the veranda. No answer. I wriggled out of my snug chrysalis and into yesterday's clothes. Using the thermos provided in the room, I made a cup of lukewarm tea and breakfasted on a mandarin orange and a handful of peanuts. This, while I studied my map of the Emei mountain area. I wondered how many other misleading directions it contained.

Outside, I indicated the plumbing problem to a boy sweeping the steps. His grin told me that I wasn't the first to point it out. I returned the grin and headed down the path to the main road. There I bore left, towards what appeared on my map to be Fuhu Temple—a nunnery the tour groups visited, that much I knew.

A boy sitting by the side of the road was cradling a Polaroid camera. His gestures invited me to have a photo taken of myself on his horse. It looked to me like a close relative of Don Quixote's Rocinantes. The boy pulled open an ancient chest full of shabby military uniforms. Caps, helmets, swords. He indicated that I should choose my disguise. He was hard to refuse.

I mounted the bony pony, swimming in a World War II Chinese general's uniform. Olive drab with crimson and gold braid. An officer's cap perched on my head. A scythe-shaped saber swung heavily from my waist. When I looked at the photo a few minutes later, I wondered if even Pat would recognize me. I tucked fifteen yuan into the boy's palm and pocketed the picture.

Leaving the main road, I followed a moss-covered rock pathway. It led alongside a stream to a pool and waterfall. A pair of spider monkeys swung down through the trees, scavenging for food. I clapped my hands and thrust my palms forward to show them I hadn't any. When they imitated me angrily, something clicked in my mind. Imitation.... Something was beginning to mesh.

Ahead loomed a wide stone staircase climbing in tiers to a temple in the distance, in the mist.

Like Wenshu Monastery in Chengdu, Fuhu Temple was lacquer-black with red and gold trim. Off the lower sanctuary were side rooms full of surprises. Lining the walls of one were jars labeled in English: ZITHER-PLAYING FROGS. They looked zitherless to me. "Do you know *How Deep is the Ocean?*" I whispered.

Another room was filled with glass cases that preserved a formidable variety of snakes. I remembered the path back to the road, heavily overgrown in spots. Where there are ex-animates, I reminded myself, surely there are animates. That brought Freddie Grimm to mind.

I entered the upper shrine, the main sanctuary. It was smokey with incense. Buttery with candlelight.

Golden Buddha statues towered over the altar, smiling at forever. Before them were two huge drums, a cauldron, and a large brass gong that reminded me of the beginning of a J. Arthur Rank production. To one side of this a nun with shaved head sat knitting.

Quilted straw pillows and mats were strewn about the floor. Occupying four of them was a quartet of Tibetan women, their red scarves winding through crow-black braids. Each time one of them went to kneel at the altar, the nun laid her work aside, picked up a thick wooden baton, struck the gong three times, then resumed her knitting.

Something led me, too, to the altar. To kneel on a quilted straw pillow. To hear the gong ring out three times for my own spirit. And then the revelation struck me. As if, in one final shake, all the pieces of the kaleidoscope had fallen into a new pattern. Mr. Yum's princesses and the *Unfinished Romance*. The Flying Dutchman and the feeble Rocinantes. Jodie Foster's dubbed voice. The monkeys, the flashcards, the battles for airline tickets. The garlic, the grime and the garbage. Even the misleading map of Emei. And above all Karen's negative hypothesis. The rite of passage was over. The initiation complete.

"Fool me once, Sally," I murmured. "But not again."

I sprang to my feet, flew out of the temple, retraced my steps back down to the main road and hurried into town to buy a bus ticket to Chengdu.

Chapter Sixteen

The bus from Emei pulled into the Chengdu station late the next afternoon. I was the first one off. I headed straight for the C.A.A.C. office. There I canceled my flight to Lhasa and bought a ticket for Hong Kong, departing Saturday, October 25 at ten-fifteen in the morning. Tomorrow.

After checking into the Jin Jiang Hotel, I first phoned the Hotel des Marronniers in Paris. Pat was not in. I left a brief message: '*Retour demain à l'Hotel Peninsula Hong Kong.*'

Next I phoned Karen's office. No, I was told, Ms. Chang was not in. In fact, she would be returning a day later than expected. On tomorrow morning's nine-thirty flight from Guilin. "Mechanical problems," the secretary added.

"I'll plan to meet Ms. Chang's plane then," I said. "But just in case we miss connections, please tell her that Paige Taylor is leaving her a jacket at the reception desk in her hotel. She'll understand."

Half an hour later the phone rang.

"Richard Kessler here."

"Now where is here?" I asked. "Hopefully not Honolulu."

"I'm being stared down by a wild-eyed ten-foot polar bear, about two seconds away from my flawless body and fragile brain."

"Mr. Kessler, be serious."

"I am! Fortunately he's been to see his taxidermist, and he now lives in a glass house. In case you haven't guessed, I'm in Anchorage airport."

"You will not go unrewarded."

"And do I have news! The dearly departed Dr. Frederick Grimm left Anchorage on Korean Air a week ago, the seventeenth to be exact. Their red-eye flight to Seoul, Tokyo, and bet you can't guess where else, but the initials are H.K."

"Same day he supposedly drifted out to sea."

"Without a paddle."

"So much for sepulchral tricks," I said wistfully. "And to think *I* nearly missed the boat!"

"Now what? Do I contact the police?"

"Not just yet. Let's find the body first."

"Make sure it was really Freddie Grimm who was on that flight?"

"Dick, I'm leaving for Hong Kong tomorrow morning."

"Hong Kong? I don't get it. What about Tibet?"

"My first guess is that Sally never left Hong Kong. My second is that she's not only greedy and crafty but vicious. And my third that she and Freddie are tangled up in something more than a dreamy little gold caper."

"Like murder one?"

"I'll phone you in the Palisades as soon as I have anything."

"But what about you? What happens when they find out—"

"That the donkey's no longer plodding after the carrot? I don't know."

"Watch yourself."

"Don't worry."

"Oh, by the way," Dick said seductively, "I thought I'd go back home via Honolulu."

"You thought wrong."

"But I could use another Hilton Mai Tai."

"Try Moët & Chandon instead. Our fridge."

"Must I?" Dick sniffed.

"You must."

O

In the morning I entrusted Karen's jacket to the reception clerk, then took a taxi to the airport. There, I went directly to the C.A.A.C. information desk. "Is the nine-thirty flight from Guilin expected to arrive on time?" I asked the agent.

"Guilin?" He nodded vaguely, as if he were trying to place it on an inner map.

"Where will the passengers be arriving?"

He pointed to a doorway.

I sat down on a bench to wait. It was five after nine. Then nine-thirty. Could I have misunderstood, I wondered? At a quarter to ten I went back to the information desk.

"Guilin?" I asked simply.

"Late," said the agent, shaking his head.

"How late?"

"Maybe ten o'clock."

"Are you sure?"

"No."

"Of course not," I said quietly. How silly of me.

At five minutes to ten a loudspeaker announced something in Chinese, and at a gate at the other end of the waiting room another agent held up a sign. It read HONG KONG.

I joined a line that trickled through the doorway, through security and customs, and outside onto the tarmac. Suddenly a familiar voice echoed in my ears.

"Paige!" Karen was clutching the far side of the fence in the baggage claim area. Her eyes were glassy, as if reality were swimming out of her ken. I stood like a rock embedded in a swift creek while my fellow passengers streamed around me, rushing towards the plane as if they were playing musical chairs again and the music had stopped.

I began to walk towards her. A flight attendant stopped me. "Customs," he said. "You go through customs, you no go back."

Karen opened her briefcase and pulled out a slim volume. Indicated a page number with her fingers. Then looked at me with drooping eyes.

The flight attendant urged me towards the aircraft. "You go now."

I nodded to Karen and walked up the stairs to the airplane door. When I turned to wave she was still clutching the fence, her head on her hands. Without Pat in my life, I probably would have tossed my ticket in the air and raced back through customs. Back to almond eyes and cherry lips that were no doubt as tender as their poetry.

I sat motionless in my window seat.

"Chengdu," I murmured. It was no longer a black dot on a map. I had touched its heart, felt it beat. It was fog and music and incense. Poetry and magic. Chengdu.... China would be Chengdu, and Chengdu would be Karen Chang.

I drew a thin volume of poems from my purse and turned to the page she had indicated.

"It is sad," I read, "for I know we'll never meet again. Now I, heartbroken, must march away under a tottering sky."

For me, there was nothing lost in the translation.

O

An hour and ten minutes later, having added not another black bow tie to my garment bag but a surprise red and white plastic fold-up set of Chinese checkers, I saw Hong Kong Island emerge beneath my window. Kowloon, Victoria Harbour, Clear Water Bay, the marinas.

In the distance I could still see the green hills of China.

Chapter Seventeen

Mr. Peng was at the reception desk at the Peninsula Hotel when I went downstairs the following morning. I greeted him with a warm hello.

"A pleasure to see you again, Mrs. Taylor." This he told me in a tone that for him, I thought, verged on emotional excess. "Shall I assume that you've found your sister?"

"Not yet, unfortunately. Shall I assume that you haven't seen her either?"

"No, Madam, I'm sorry to say."

I found myself staring at the calendar on the wall behind him. Today was Sunday, October 26.

I turned to Mr. Peng. "My sister arrived in Hong Kong on Sunday, September 28. Exactly four weeks ago."

"Yes, Madam?"

"Is it still true that non-residents are allowed to stay in Hong Kong for only one month at a time?" I asked.

"Quite true, Madam. But that's really no problem. It's so convenient to go to Macao for a quick exit-reentry."

"There's no airport there, is there?"

"No. You can go only by sea, but it's a short trip. Very pleasant. Hydrofoil, jetfoil, high-speed ferry, steamer. Most leave from the Shun Tak Centre wharf."

"Thank you." I handed Mr. Peng my room key. "I'm in a bit of a rush," I said, and bolted for the door.

○

The white-haired man at the Shun Tak Ferry ticket office did not recognize anyone in the pictures I showed him. Nor did any of the hydrofoil companies' personnel. I moved on to a young man behind the Hong Lok jetfoil ticket window.

"I'm trying to find my sister and her husband. They said they were going to Macao." I placed two photos on the counter. "Have you seen them? Perhaps in the last day or two?"

His eyes bored through thick glasses to devour Sally Barrett, first as Cinderella, then as bathing beauty. "Oh, yes," he replied without hesitation. He looked up at me with the same devouring smile. "Sister also very pretty."

"They were here?"

"She was."

"This man was with her?" I indicated Freddie Grimm.

"No. No, no. Other man."

"What did he look like?"

The young man shrugged. "Tall, like this one. Maybe more...skinny. Maybe hair straight like Chinese."

"Maybe." I wondered if the agent took less interest in identifying the male of the species. Or was the man perhaps the Marc Sancerre to whom Sally had shipped the sailing gear? "When were they here?" was my next question.

"This morning. Maybe two, three hours ago."

"And they bought tickets for Macao?"

"Hong Lok jetfoil. The best."

I removed a bill from my wallet. "I'd like to buy a ticket also, please."

"Boat in twenty minutes. You will go first to customs."

"I appreciate your help."

○

An hour and a half later I stepped off the jetfoil onto a pier in the peninsular Portuguese Colony of Macao. My watch told me it was almost three. I took the steps up to the office of the Department of Tourism two at a time. An attractive dark-skinned woman with distinct Iberian features stepped from behind a desk to greet me. A crimson flower bloomed in her hair. Dangling golden earrings bounced against her neck. She gave me a gypsy's smile and a contralto's hello. I wasn't at all surprised to read CARMEN on her nameplate.

"I'm very anxious to find two friends of mine," I told her. "I know they arrived in Macao today, but I have no idea where they're staying. Or for how long." I showed her the photos of Sally and Freddie. "Did they by chance reserve a hotel room with you?"

"No, I'm sorry," Carmen answered. "I haven't seen them. They probably booked from Hong Kong. If you like, you may use our telephone to call the hotels. There aren't that many that tourists stay in here."

I looked across the room at a WELCOME TO MACAO sign on a display table stacked with pamphlets.

"Thank you, but if I may have a hotel directory brochure and a map, I'll go directly to the hotels," I said. "I want to surprise them. Where do you think new jetsetters might spend the night?"

"Are they gamblers?" Carmen asked.

"Of a sort, yes."

"The Lisboa Hotel has a casino. The Oriental too. Many have nightclubs and discos. The Hyatt Regency on Taipa Island. The Royal, Presidente. You'll have to try them all. I personally think the Pousada de São Tiago is especially nice." Carmen paused before adding, "For lovers. Probably *your* kind of place, too."

I thanked her, then headed outside and hailed a taxi. I related my mission to the driver. He was a beefy man with an unlighted cigarette butt built into one corner of his mouth. He seemed delighted with the prospect of a change of pace.

First stop was the nearest hotel, the Lisboa. But no Grimms, Barretts or Sancerres were registered there. And none of the receptionists could recognize anyone in my photos. On my way out, I strayed briefly into a game room filled with one-armed bandits and wall-to-wall people. My ears rang with the sound of metal coins raining into plastic containers. No, I thought, Sally and Crew should at least be into baccarat or chemin de fer. Roulette, perhaps, and more likely the Russian variety.

The Taipa Island Hyatt revealed no evidence of the pursued either. Nor did eight other hotels on the peninsula.

Leaving the Rua da Palha, the taxi jolted down a narrow cobblestone street, redolent with olive oil and fried fish. Highrises in the background vied for attention with the older buildings that spilled over onto the uneven strip of sidewalk. They were a colorful chaos of shapes and angles that housed the poor, that fed them, entertained them, and gave them a dim place to work. Above, out windows and across rooftops, were strung pieces of laundry. I watched them flutter in the breeze like Buddhist prayer flags from a Nepalese temple. Perhaps they too send messages up to heaven, I was thinking, when the driver rerouted my stream of consciousness.

He pointed to the top of a long, graceful, sweeping stone staircase. "São Paulo Cathedral."

I tilted my head out the taxi window. Only the facade of the structure remained, and above it only silent gray cannons on the austere walls of a once impregnable citadel.

"You like visit?" he asked.

"Yes, but not now," I told him. "One day soon though," I added, thinking how Pat would love this odd bit of Europe drifted into the Orient. My fleeting fantasy saw us arm in arm, wandering the cobblestone streets.

The taxi wove in and out of traffic down the Avenida da Republica, spun around the tip of Macao peninsula and swerved to the curb in front of the cave-like entranceway to the converted Fortaleza da Barra. The Pousada de São Tiago.

Stone stairs led up through a rocky tunnel. Its unique walls dripped with cool water. I emerged into the reception room above. The decor was Portuguese colonial—dark polished wood, wrought-iron grillwork, leaded windows. Outside were quiet terraces, pink tile roofs, walls draped with bougainvillea, balconies scarlet with geraniums. In the distance I could see the delta and the bay, spotted with sampans and junks. I was enchanted. Yes, I thought, Carmen was right. If this isn't a place for lovers, none exists on this earth.

No one in reception, however, could identify either Sally Barrett or Freddie Grimm.

I checked my watch. A few minutes past eight. I stepped out onto the adjacent terrace. The al fresco Cafe da Barra gleamed with white patio chairs and tables set in cool circles of shade under sea-green umbrellas. In a doorway a clutch of waiters, arms folded, waited for the next signal from a customer. I approached them, took a photo from my purse.

"Pardon me, but would any of you by chance recognize this woman?"

"I do, yes," the graying headwaiter answered unhesitantly. "I waited on her and her husband this afternoon. They had a late lunch here." He pointed to a private corner table near the stone railing. "Sat right over there."

"What about this man?" I placed my index finger on Freddie. "Was he with her?"

"No. Just the two of them."

"Could you describe her husband for me?"

"Oh, more slender than this man. Darker. Very nice man," he added. His smile indicated a very nice tip.

"Are they perhaps staying here at the Pousada?"

"I don't think so. They didn't sign their bill."

"They paid in cash?"

"Yes." He nodded approval.

"Thank you so much."

For a brief second I wondered what kind of lovers would forgo a night here. Then I flew down the rock steps of the Pousada to the waiting taxi.

"Back to the pier, quickly," I told my driver. "For some reason my friends have hurried back to Hong Kong."

"Too late now. Last jetfoil already gone." He caught my eyes in the rear view mirror. "You still want to go?"

"Yes."

The androgynous official at the ticket office confirmed my fears. A woman fitting Sally Barrett's description had left for Hong Kong on the last boat.

"How long ago?" I asked.

"Over an hour."

"So she's already back in Hong Kong?"

The official nodded.

"When is the next jetfoil?"

"Tomorrow morning."

"Tomorrow morning?"

"Hydrofoils, ferries, all will be booked for the evening or finished for the day."

"Finished?"

"Finished. *Finito. Fini.* Go see for yourself."

Outside, the taxi driver was leaning against his cab, toying with his rosary. He lifted his shoulders in an I-told-you-so-but-I'm-sorry gesture.

Fifteen minutes later we were back at the Pousada de São Tiago. I checked into a room with a balcony heady with gardenias, and a bed large enough to accommodate a cast of four.

I waited nearly half an hour for an open telephone line to California. A series of buzzes, clicks, cut-offs and wrong numbers finally deadended in a booming voice that said, "Richard Kessler here."

"And Paige Taylor here."

"Which is where?"

"Macao. Where I am currently retooling my tale without a toothbrush."

"And becoming incoherent. I thought you were going to Hong Kong."

"I did. But we can skip my itinerary. Do remind me, though, to tell you about my ties. I have one for you."

"Mai Tais?"

"Listen, Dick, I have major news. Sally was here. Today. In Macao. I just missed her by a couple of hours."

"Awesome! Freddie with her?"

"No. But some other man is. Perhaps the Marc Sancerre she mailed the sailing gear to."

"Maybe Freddie's looking for her?" Dick ventured.

"Who knows? Anyway, I'm stranded here for the night. Any news there?"

"Bill tells me that Metropolitan Life is about to open an investigation. They want to know all about his late partner. In fact, GG got a call yesterday from a guy named Brandt. He was asking about Carole Oliver, too."

"Tell Bill and GG to avoid him if they can. I don't need somebody else complicating things. Something has to give here, and soon. I'll buzz you tomorrow from Hong Kong."

"Hey, hold on," Dick said. "In case you still take an interest in my career, I'm auditioning tonight. A musical. Westlake Community Theater."

"Again? Not another Gilbert and Sullivan?"

"You got it."

"Not *HMS Pinafore*?"

"Close. *The Pirates of Penzance*."

Oh, ye gods, I thought, as I wished him success.

○

The next voice told me, "*Oui, Madame Towne est dans sa chambre. Ne quittez pas.*"

When Pat answered, I gave her a throaty, "I ham cray-zee forrr yourrr boddy."

"It is now covered with the most lovely red roses, for which I thank you, my dear, sweet Paige. And it's waiting for you."

"I hope it won't have to wait much longer," I said. "I have news. Our Dick has found out that Freddie Grimm outlived his obituary. Slipped out of Anchorage, destination Hong Kong. Either that or someone's impersonating him, just like someone's been impersonating Sally in China."

"Wheee! Well, I can match that. At the Sorbonne, I uncovered Sally Romanski's address in Paris. From her college days. Rue La Condamine. Near Place Clichy."

"Brava!"

"I interviewed her former landlady. Would you believe a Madame Sancerre?"

"Would I!"

"And—my dear Paige, I trust my reward will be here on earth and not in some remote heaven—guess what? It was her son, Marc, who cooperated in Sally's pregnancy! She remembers Mademoiselle Romanski as being a very intense student up until spring vacation. That's when her son came up from Cannes to visit. Hadn't been home in months. He was working on some Haitian millionaire's yacht. Sailing the seven seas. That's why Marc's visits were so rare."

"And now?"

"She has seen him only once in the last two years—for a few hours one afternoon last January."

"January? Sally was in Paris in January!"

"For a last tango, maybe?"

"Did Madame Sancerre mention any other contact with Marc?"

"All she gets is an occasional postcard from him. She blames it all on his girlfriend."

"Sally?"

"No. Some French woman. A Suzanne somebody. They didn't hit it off at all, she and Madame Sancerre. Anyway, Suzanne was working as a cook. Guess where?"

"Don't tell me she and Marc were in the same boat?"

"Bingo! Also, his last postcard came in August, from California. Marc wrote that he and Suzanne were married and were getting a yacht of their own!"

"Pat, your deeds will be immortalized!"

"And now for the *pièce de résistance*. Madame Sancerre had a picture of Marc and Suzanne that he had sent her a few years ago. The two of them basking in the sunshine on the deck of a sailboat. Coconut palms leaning into the background."

"What will you take for that photo?"

"You should have it at the Peninsula Hotel tomorrow morning. French Express."

"How am I ever going to thank you for this one?"

"I'll tell you some time. But it's a bit much for a public phone."

"Well, I would hope so," I murmured. I went on to elaborate on my revelation in Emei and my trip back to Hong Kong, and to explain my presence now in Macao.

Pat listened carefully to my story, then said, "Please, sweetheart, get some backup. It's time. I know we have an understanding to respect each other's decisions in life and to give the other plenty of space to act them out as she wishes. But in this case, if Sally and Company went to a good deal of trouble to mislead you, what do you suppose they would do if they find out you're on to them?"

"I'll be careful."

"Backup," Pat repeated.

"Soon, soon."

After we finally said good-bye, I made one last phone call.

"Room service," answered a cheery voice.

I was studying a menu on the desk before me. "I'd like to order one Caldo Verde and one Galinha à Portuguesa," I said. "And a chilled bottle of Lancer's rosé."

"Service for one?" the voice wanted to know.

"Yes," I replied. "Unfortunately."

I wandered out onto the balcony and leaned against the wrought-iron railing. Far out in the bay, a sleek schooner with orange and white striped sails was tacking west into the sunset. I followed it until it disappeared into a tiny cove on the mainland—until the green hills of China above it became curvacious shadows in the gathering darkness.

Chapter Eighteen

I entered the lobby of the Peninsula Hotel a little after ten the next morning. Mr. Peng was standing behind the reception counter.

"Good morning, Mrs. Taylor." He glumly dangled a key in front of me.

I took it. "Caught overnight in Macao," I said sheepishly.

Mr. Peng stooped to retrieve something from beneath the counter. It was a large red, white and blue envelope covered with stamps.

"This came for you," he told me stiffly. "About five minutes ago."

I thanked him, stepped aside and opened it. Inside, a glossy five-by-seven color print exposed a well tanned couple in bikinis. Arms around each other, they were sitting on a circle of thick rope on the deck of a yacht. The man looked to be in his early thirties. Tall, slender and sinewy, with unmistakably Gallic features. His straight black hair was ruffled by a recent swim and a breeze. The woman was perhaps seven or eight years younger. A leggy, dark-eyed brunette. I thought I recognized Port-au-Prince in the background.

I turned to Mr. Peng, who was looking as discreetly as possible over my shoulder. "I'll bet you recognize this woman."

"Isn't that your sister?"

"Yes." I handed him my room key and a gargantuan smile. "I have to run."

Outside, I hailed a taxi. It was exactly forty minutes past noon when I entered Marine Police Headquarters in Tsim Sha Tsui. I told the receptionist that I had important information regarding drug trafficking in the harbor and was directed to a Captain Yee's office on the second floor.

There I spoke with a pleasant Eurasian woman whose desk bore the nameplate SERGEANT SUYIN. "Captain Yee is out to lunch right now," she told me. "But he should be back in a few moments, if you'd like to wait."

"Thank you, I would."

Sergeant Suyin motioned me to a row of chocolate-swirl vinyl chairs. "Please have a seat."

I had read the backwards circular lettering on the door— MARINE POLICE | HONG KONG —at least twenty times before it was pushed open by a small, wiry, middle-aged man. His taffy polo shirt was unbuttoned at the neck, its collar curled like a pair of dried leaves. His navy blue trousers dragged the floor. Their matching baggy suitcoat rested precariously on his shoulders. I couldn't believe it. A Chinese Colombo.

"Captain Yee, Paige Taylor to see you." The Sergeant squinted into her word processor. "About an urgent matter."

I took the hand he offered and studied his face. The only moving parts were the eyes. Eyes like acorns. Yee returned the scrutiny for one long moment. His left thumb and index finger pulled meditatively on his right ear. Then his mouth curled slightly into something like the tilde in español. This, I supposed, indicated a smile.

"Come in," he said abruptly, his mouth moving no more than a ventriloquist's. The tilde vanished as quickly as it had come.

Yee carefully hung his coat over the back of his chair while I admired the wall behind him. It was papered in blue and white navigational charts, with handwritten notes thumbtacked here and there.

With a "Please!" he waved me into an armchair on the far side of a cluttered oak desk. When his eyes had again fixed on mine, he nodded thoughtfully. "Blue, but not South China Sea," he said. "No. Not Indian Ocean either." Captain Yee paused again. "Mediterranean," he concluded. "Mediterranean blue."

I decided against a comment about acorns and smiled instead. "I come to you about a matter of utmost urgency," I said. I handed him my business card and a small eelskin folder containing my license.

"A private investigator?"

"Looking for a woman named Sally Barrett. She left California last month after relieving her husband, Dr. Barrett, of something in the neighborhood of half a million dollars. I traced her to Hong Kong. Then followed someone who, I think, was posing as Mrs. Barrett into China, only to guess later on that I was being led on a wild goose chase. Now I have every reason to believe that she's still here, and in the company of a former lover. A Frenchman named Marc Sancerre.

"Her husband's business partner, Dr. Frederick Grimm, also disappeared from California recently. The police there believe he was killed in some drug operation. But my assistant has discovered that Grimm, or someone posing as him, left Alaska about a week ago on a flight bound for Hong Kong. To complicate matters, Dr. Barrett's former receptionist, Carole Oliver, and the father of his next door neighbor, Manuel Mandariaga, were both found dead a month before his wife's disappearance. My guess is that both were murdered, and that they have some connection to the Grimm and Barrett case. I'll be happy to give you the details."

Yee asked, "Would you like a cup of tea?"

"That would be lovely."

"*Chà*," he mumbled to the intercom, and to me, "Please go on." He folded his hands on the desk and waited.

"I suspect that either Freddie Grimm was and is in touch with Sally Barrett, or is after her for some other reason. The plot appears to be more complicated than I originally thought, and perhaps quite dangerous."

"*Ménages à trois* are always dangerous," Yee said. "So you are trying to locate both Mrs. Barrett and Dr. Grimm?"

"Along with Marc Sancerre and Mrs. Barrett's impersonator, whom I believe to be his wife, Suzanne."

Captain Yee responded to a knock at the door and returned to his desk with a tray bearing a rose-flowered teapot and two saucerless, handleless cups.

"Green tea," he announced, offering me one. "No sugar."

"Thank you."

"You have not yet involved the police in California?"

"No. These people may not only be hard to catch up with but impossible to bring to justice if they have any suspicion that someone is on to them. But I thought the time had come to alert you, because I may need police support soon." I riveted Yee with my Mediterranean blues. "Someone with a creative mind, great imagination, and a vision in this case that imposes silence."

The officer's mouth curled into another tilde before he said, "A man like Captain Yee."

"Exactly."

"How do I know you're legitimate?"

"The Babcock Detective Agency in San Francisco can vouch for both my credentials and my credibility. But I must ask you to keep my present mission between us." I paused to sip my tea. "How do I know I can trust *you*?"

My sly grin was lost on Yee. He drained his cup, leaned back in his chair, propped his feet up on the desk, and with his right thumb and index finger pulled gently on his left ear. "Why Marine Police?"

I replaced my teacup on the tray. "It seems quite likely that a sailing vessel of some sort is involved. My guess is that at least two of the cast of characters are living on it."

"So first you want to locate this imagined vessel?"

"Yes. Would Marine Police have registration information?"

"We have access only to the names of persons with a vessel registered in Hong Kong," Yee replied. "Of course customs has information concerning the entry and exit of all vessels."

"Shall I assume that anyone planning to depart must first notify the Port Authority?" I asked. "File a float plan?"

Yee nodded.

"And if nothing surfaces in any of the above," I went on, "I suppose looking for them in the marinas, yacht clubs, typhoon shelters or whatever would be quite a project?"

Yee's answer was to gather his short legs under him and head for a series of floor-to-ceiling cabinets across the room. He pulled one open, withdrew a stack of charts, picked out half a dozen and spread them on the office floor.

"You have three basic territories: mainland Hong Kong, Lantau Island, Hong Kong Island." Yee traced the jagged shoreline with a yardstick. "More yacht harbors on the eastern part than the western."

"So many places for them to hide," I murmured.

"Around here," Yee went on, "past Kai Tak, Clear Water Bay. On up into these coves. Hebe Haven Yacht Club here. Sai Kung, High Island, Tai Long Wan. Tolo Harbour. Up here, Plover Cove. Then down the Deep Bay side. The New Territories. Anchorages around here. And the islands."

I was awed by the possibilities. "And time is running out," I said under my breath.

Yee moved the yardstick to a separate map of Hong Kong Island. "Royal Hong Kong Yacht Club. A major typhoon shelter in Causeway Bay. And the Aberdeen Marina, of course, if you're looking for jet-setters."

I finally recovered myself enough to respond, "Yes, I see what you mean."

Yee leaned on his yardstick, scrutinizing me and pulling on his right ear again. Then his mouth formed its peculiar little curl. "Let's try registration first."

I answered his smile with a curl of my own. "I appreciate your tea and sympathy."

○

I lay sprawled on my bed in the Peninsula Hotel. "Marine Police had no vessel registered to a Grimm, Barrett or Sancerre," I said into the creamy phone receiver. "Nor has any entered Hong Kong in the past few months. Or filed a float plan."

Dick asked, "Did you try Lee Roman?"

"Roman and Romanski both. Zero. And Yee has assured me that if any of the above are by chance staying in a Hong Kong hotel, Sergeant Suyin will soon know about it."

"But if there really is a boat in all this, it's registered in some other name?"

"Or recently purchased without the name change having gone through Marine Police yet. Unlikely, according to Yee. So I've been entertaining myself at the marinas with my little photo collection. And getting nowhere."

"How are you getting past private clubhouses and such?" Dick wanted to know. "I thought the P word in Hong Kong was Privacy."

"With an instant-print box of new business cards and a string of non sequiturs."

"The kind that come so naturally to me?"

"The same." I asked, "Any news there?"

"I had a 'please contact' message on my voice mail today from Metropolitan Life."

"Which you ignored."

"Naturally. According to Bill, their Agent Brandt has been quizzing him about you. Brandt knows that you're in Hong Kong. Of course he thinks you're only after Sally."

"But he may soon put Freddie in the picture. Meanwhile, we're the only ones who know about him, right?"

"And Pat," Dick said. "Remember her? Pat Towne?"

"As a matter of fact, I tried to reach her earlier, but the lines were jammed. It may be awhile before I can get through to her. I'm leaving here as soon as I can load my new briefcase with some magazines. Back to Hebe Haven Bay and on up around the shoreline to Sai Kung."

"Magazines?"

"Catch up with Pat, will you, Dick? Tell her that I'm certain it was Suzanne who was leading me around China. Keeping the carrot just the right distance from the donkey."

"But why?"

"To have Sally Barrett disappear somewhere in Tibet or India, I suspect, and never be heard from again. The mistake was to pick a flight path that was so obviously not for Sally's kind of solo."

"I know: 'the grime, the garbage, the garlic.'"

I asked, "How's GG doing?"

"Doing everything but wearing a black arm band. I did manage to get her to have lunch with me yesterday."

"Good. And Bill?"

"He tells me he's into 'low-maintenance' relationships now."

"One-night stands, in other words."

"You got that right. He had one at his house last night. A real tomato, as Philip Marlowe might say."

"Dick, I want you to check out car rentals in the name of Marc Sancerre for the time around Carole Oliver's death. Pat said Madame Sancerre's postcard from him last August came from California. If you come up with anything, get Lieutenant Bashore to check it out."

"The chlorine connection?"

"Right." I hesitated, then asked, "What about your Gilbert & Sullivan audition?"

"It was postponed 'til tomorrow," Dick answered. "By the way, I'm considering a new stage name. What do you think about Richard Chrysler?"

"Kessler to Chrysler?"

"Don't you think it's classier?"

"Whiskey and ribs to cars?" I paused, watching the blips racing across my inner screen. As soon as I said, "What about Ford Dodge?" I was sorry.

Dick was silent. Finally he asked, almost inaudibly, "I should keep thinking?"

"I would," I said quietly.

O

I headed down to the lobby early the following morning, prepared for another round of marinas. I greeted Mr. Peng with a pleasant hello and handed him my room key.

"Good morning, Madam." Mr. Peng's voice now teetered on the edge of scorn. He held out a small pink envelope. "A telephone message just came for you. Perhaps you were in the elevator."

"Thank you."

I flipped open the envelope and read: "Please phone Captain Yee, Hong Kong Marine Police." I smiled wanly at

Mr. Peng. His countenance emanated omniscience as he dangled my room key back over the counter. I returned to my room and dialed Yee's office.

"No question about it," Yee began. "My staff worked all night. There is no Grimm or Barrett registered in any hotel in the area. Or Sancerre either. Other than a Mildred Barrett," he added. "Staying at the Prince Hotel. A dowager empress according to my Sergeant Suyin. On a seven-day shopping tour to Hong Kong with thirty-three other senior citizens from Florida. And in no mood for questions at two in the morning. Not *your* Mrs. Barrett."

"No. I don't think Sally's *that* good at disguises."

"That complicates things, perhaps?"

"Or perhaps simplifies them." I thought a moment. "Captain Yee, would you mind faxing me that list of vessels recently registered in Hong Kong?"

"No problem. I'll have it at your hotel within the hour. But I can assure you that my staff has gone over it thoroughly."

"Thanks. I'll check back with you this afternoon."

I replaced the receiver in its cradle and lay back on the bed. My heart wasn't with my briefcase and my new business cards. I decided to try phoning Pat again. No answer. I pulled a pillow over my head.

A few minutes later I picked up the phone and asked for directory assistance in Paris. They had a listed number for a J. Sancerre on Rue la Condamine. I tried it. A major mistake. Madame Sancerre had been sleeping, did not appreciate being disturbed, and had no idea whatsoever what the maiden name was of her son's wife, Suzanne. Nor did she care to know. *Did I hear*?

That really made my day. I gathered my purse and briefcase and charged down to the lobby. Mr. Peng handed me a manilla envelope and took my room key in exchange. My smile was straight out of Dick's method acting manual.

Chapter Nineteen

It was mid-morning when I looked down the road from the bus stop near the entrance to Seahorse Harbour above Clear Water Bay. There was no taxi in sight, but a red double-decker Number 92 bus came swaying towards me at full tilt. I wagged an arm, and it lurched to a halt.

I dropped three coins into the glass and metal container next to the driver, climbed up to the top deck and sat down by the front window. Jungle-green hills rolled away in all directions. Over them, the jagged mountainous mainland. And above that, torn patches of blue in murky skies. I hoped it wouldn't rain.

The next circle on my map was the Rock Point Yacht Club. I got off at the stop across the road from it and found my way into the empty clubhouse. Only a faint odor of soy sauce and beer greeted me. My wits were getting duller by the moment.

I noticed a handwritten memo on a bulletin board and entertained myself by reading it aloud: "Crew of three sought for cruise to the Maldives in 52′ sloop. Experience essential." Maybe I should apply?

A singsong voice interrupted my reverie.

"May I help you?" A well fed young man in a crisp white short-sleeved shirt and black bow tie and trousers stood in the doorway.

I stared momentarily at the tie before I said, "Actually, yes. My name is Caitlin Queeg." I handed him a white business card. Within the midnight blue outline of a five-masted clipper ship, three printed lines told him that I was the assistant editor of *Nautilus* magazine and that I had an impressive address at the Hopewell Center on Hong Kong Island. "Are you the manager?"

"Mr. Lee, Assistant Manager," he answered. "Manager away for today. Sorry," he added, "but I cannot recognize the name of your magazine."

I pulled a copy of *Cruising World* out of my briefcase. "How about this one?" I asked.

"Oh, yes. Many of our people get *Cruising World*."

"Well, we're new. We're their competition. Now, I don't want to bother anybody. Management *or* boat people. I just want to send them one little copy of *Nautilus*. Free, of course." I eyed Lee for approval.

"Of course."

"No strings attached—just to have a look at. We're going to have *fabulous* ads! Wait 'til you see our fold-out color spread of straw hats by Tristes Tropiques! You'll want to buy one yourself! Who knows what a treasury of information someone might find in the personals?" I pointed over my shoulder at the bulletin board behind me. "Like somebody looking for a crew."

I am boring myself silly, I was thinking, as Lee nodded agreement.

"If you'll give me your list of names and slip numbers, I'll see to it that each and every one of your people receives a copy of *Nautilus* in next month's mail. You too, if you like."

"Yes. I read English pretty well now."

"Our literary style is utter simplicity," I told him, not even ashamed of myself.

"Please, come with me."

Mr. Lee led me into his office. There he presented me with his roster. Was there a Grimm, Barrett or Sancerre on it? Of course not. I moved on to Act Two. That was my mini photo collection, which I spread on Mr. Lee's desk. He recognized no one. Act Three: I was outside, sitting on a bench at the bus stop. In no hurry for a bus. Or a taxi either. I opened the manilla envelope from Captain Yee and began scanning the registration lists he had faxed me.

"Einsdorf, Helmut," I read aloud. Hebe Haven Yacht Club. The right hand column gave the name of the vessel registered to him: MEIN KAMPH. I wondered if Helmut wore a little black mustache as well.

Hershey, Donald, caught my eye. Vessel: BOOMERANG. Australian, I supposed. This was getting to be fun.

I imagined each vessel as I went along. CHINA DOLL. Ho hum. PUSSY POWER. Tee hee. YACHTSIE TOTTSIE. Oh, please. MADE IN HONG KONG. Really! KOSHER NOSTRA. KOSHER NOSTRA? I laughed aloud.

And then, there it was. HERE LIES THE HEART. The street where the heart lies! Rue Gît-le-coeur! Suddenly I saw spring-time in Paris, and Sally and Marc roaming the Latin Quarter in search of some special space to celebrate their budding love.

My eyes flicked from the right to the left hand column. The registered owner(s): Prévost, S. & partners. Vessel berthed in Club Marina Cove.

I looked down the road, but there was still no taxi in sight. I dug in my briefcase for the marina map Yee had given me with bus routes marked on it. Then studied the numbers of the buses on the post at the bus stop. Ten minutes later a Number 91 red double-decker which read SAI KUNG collected me. It was the noon hour and overflowing. I stood near the rear door, hugging my briefcase, for the run to Club Marina Cove.

The manager was a pushover. An Englishman, Barrie Dudley, with Peter O'Toole eyes and a Guinness nose. I gave him a synopsis of my *Nautilus* story and we were soon sipping orange tea in his office and looking at the roster. Yes, the yacht HERE LIES THE HEART in slip Number 43 was registered to

Prévost, Suzanne. Marc Sancerre, Sally Barrett and Frederick Grimm were also listed as on board.

I phoned the yacht from the public phone booth outside the clubhouse. A man with a heavy French accent answered. I gave him a story with a string of non sequiturs that Dick would have been proud of. I wove it into my magazine tale and asked to speak with Frederick Grimm.

"He went into Sai Kung," I was told. More story-telling got me: "To the fish market."

I boarded another Number 91 double-decker and rode it to the end of the line.

It was almost two o'clock by the time the bus had emptied out in Sai Kung. The narrow street I followed towards the harbor was lined with small shops and unassuming eateries. Places with names like Wah Fu Company and the Dragon Boat Restaurant. Balconies above them were hung with laundry, drying slowly in the humid October breeze.

The putt-putt-putt of motorized sampans announced the waterfront. The odor of fresh fish led me towards the wet market.

I found the fish tanks fascinating. Writhing with eels, crawling with crabs. Stunning pink crabs with Aegean-blue claws. Giant lobsters. Rust and sapphire. Emerald. Jade.

"Two catties of the large prawns, please," a man behind me told the fishmonger.

I turned around in slow motion. Removed my sunglasses. I stood face-to-face with Freddie Grimm.

"Only two?" I asked quietly. "These must be grim times."

Freddie's eyes blinked instant terror. His body arched, calves taut, mouth breathless. For a moment I was sure he was going to bolt. Then his facial muscles slackened and he resumed breathing.

"Can we talk?" I asked, in a Joan Rivers voice.

"Do I have a choice?"

It was high time for a fat lie. I said, "Marine Police already have Club Marina Cove under surveillance. Take us somewhere where we can talk."

Freddie surrendered with a simple shrug. He handed the fishmonger a bill and grabbed the dark green plastic sack of prawns neatly tied with seaweed. I followed him through the back alleys of Sai Kung into a quiet square and inside Pebbles Restaurant. It reminded me of an old Bogart film—bamboo tables and chairs, potted plants, an overhead fan stiring the air ever so slightly.

"'Ello, luv," the buxom blonde waitress said to Freddie in what I recognized as East London brogue. "Wot can I get you?"

We both ordered Beefeater gin and tonic and settled into a rear table hidden from view of the front door and bar by a sprawling rubber plant.

Freddie mumbled, "How the hell did you find me?"

"*You* answer the questions," I said flatly. "We know the basic story. Now I want the details, and don't waste my time. Unless you want to grow old with a male roommate."

He cracked a knuckle. "Guess I don't have much to lose."

"Nothing. But you do have a good deal to gain. Cooperation and indemnity go together like...shall we say...gin and tonic?"

Freddie pushed both hands through his thick, wavy hair, from his forehead to the nape of his neck. He paused, then drew a deep breath and blew it up towards the overhead fan. "Where do I start?"

"Why not do an *Alice in Wonderland* number," I suggested. "Begin at the beginning and go right through to the end."

"It was a harmless scheme," he began, his voice liquid guilt. "I had no intention of hurting anybody. Bill Barrett was to get my half of the partnership—all my clients, naturally.

Worth a small fortune! Bill's a workaholic anyway. He'll always earn far more than he'll ever spend. As for GG...I tried to be fair. I got the house paid for and left her a fat life insurance policy. She's a hell of a lot better off than if I'd divorced her, that's for sure. She has nothing to worry about for the rest of her life."

"*Had*," I corrected him.

"Had," Freddie repeated sullenly. "Is she all right?"

"Would you be all right?"

He stared up at the fan.

"Why did you do it, Freddie?"

His answer was a defensive, "I was in love!"

"'Ere you are, luv." The waitress put two glasses brimful of gin and tonic on the table. "Cheers!"

"Cheers!" I raised my glass to her, then turned to Freddie. "You were saying?"

He gulped his drink, staring up at the fan. "Life with GG was...well...I guess white bread would say it all. The sparks went out years ago. What few there were. But I do love her." His tone softened. "Really I do. It's just that...well...Sal was something else. The kind that makes you see stars. No mountain too high. No ocean too deep." Freddie looked me in the eye for the first time. "You know?"

"Yes, I know."

He paused long enough for his stare to turn defiant. "Why should I tell you all this? Why should I incriminate myself?"

"You already have. The day you smeared blood on your car seat." I tasted my drink. "But I'm thinking of a friendly District Attorney I could contact in Los Angeles—if you're prepared to tell the whole truth. And I think I could convince GG not to press charges.... Let's hear it, Freddie."

He pondered the fan again. "I met Sal a couple of years ago," he began, sounding now like his tongue had suddenly doubled in size. "Almost to the day. It was Halloween, as a matter of fact. GG and I had tickets for the Music Center. San Francisco Opera. A double-header. *Cavalleria Rusticana* and *I Pagliacci*. But she wasn't feeling well, so I went alone. And then along came Sally."

"And sat down beside you."

"And invited me to a midnight party afterward. I couldn't help myself. Marina del Rey. Some punker she knew had a boat there. Funky kind of party. Bunch of space cadets."

Funny, how Freddie seemed to be relaxing. Talking to me as if I were his therapist and he needed to unload. Maybe the guilt had gotten to him already. I said, "And?"

"We started seeing each other. Sal always wanted to live on a sailboat. There was one for rent in Newport Beach. I took it for her. We'd meet there evenings, weekends, whatever. Whenever. I was mad about her. I'd never met anybody like Sal. Never! I loved sailing, too. I was already licensed to handle anything up to forty-five feet. Hell, I wanted her dream just as badly as she did." Freddie drained his glass. "And that's about it."

"'It' meaning Prologue. Now let's get into Chapter One."

"One?"

"Let's hear it."

Freddie studied the sliver of lemon rind in the bottom of his glass. "It was going to take money. The dream, that is. A million bucks, Sal figured. At best I could come up with only half of that."

"So she got you to introduce her to Bill Barrett. And, as Bill would say, chemistry did the rest."

He nodded in slow motion.

"The whole marriage was a set-up?"

Freddie nodded again. "One year after we met. To the day."

"Halloween. I know. Let's move into Chapter Two."

"Sal figured it would take another year to get everything into Krugerrands. Get the dream boat lined up. Make things look right." Freddie made wet circles on the table with his empty glass. "You know that song that goes 'If it takes forever, I will wait for you—'"

"*Umbrellas of Cherbourg.*"

"Sal used to sing it all the time."

"What about this dream boat?"

"I need another drink," he said. "How about you?"

I shook my head.

Freddie stood, held up one finger to the waitress, collapsed in his chair again. Silent.

I goaded him on with, "I'm listening. But I'm growing older and crankier by the minute."

"It all seemed so simple," he sighed. "Sal figured half a million for the yacht, half a million or so to invest and live on while we sailed the world. The Good Life. Forever."

"And ever. Amen."

"'If you're feeling fancy free, come and wander through the world with me.'" Freddie made a lame effort to sing. "That's another one of her favorites," he said. "'And in winter we'll drink summer wine.'" His voice cracked.

"'Wine' as in 'you'll be mine,'" I murmured, seeing his eyes begin to glisten.

The waitress exchanged Freddie's empty glass for a full one. "Drink up, luv," she told me with a wink.

I winked back and took another sip of my gin and tonic. By that time Freddie had pulled himself together. I said, "Tell me about the yacht."

"Well, I was damned busy at the office," he began again. "But Sal had the time to check everything out and plan our moves. The best solution, she figured, was to have the dream boat built by Cheoy Lee—a shipyard here in Hong Kong. A motorsailer. Sixty-three footer." His voice grew a protective coat of arrogance. "Teak decks. The works. Double-masted beauty. Push-button controls. Diesel oil tanks that hold close to two thousand gallons. Enough to cross any body of water on this planet without depending on the sails."

"Down payment somewhere in the neighborhood of one hundred thousand?" I guessed. "The first stash of Kruger-rands? Cashed out in Tijuana?"

"You know that too? Okay. Yes. Close to it."

"Sally needed a middleman for the deal. Who was that?"

"She was writing to various people, places, making connections, getting prices—"

"Using a P.O. box in Brentwood."

"What *don't* you know?"

"What did she decide on?"

"She put an ad in *Cruising World* for two crew members. Somebody based in Hong Kong who could handle other business for us, too. Got tons of replies. But one of them was a real surprise." Freddie managed a shadow of a smile. "From a guy Sal had met years ago. In fact, when she was a student in Paris, she'd rented a room from his mother. A guy she knew she could really trust. A guy able and willing to do just about anything."

"A jock of all trades?" I couldn't help but murmur.

"He and his wife had worked on yachts for years. The perfect pair for us."

"That would be Marc Sancerre? And Suzanne Prévost? And you thought using her family name for marine registration would hide your tracks?" I took the photo Pat had sent out of my purse. "Do these two look familiar?"

Freddie stared at it, his lips slack.

"Where was Sally supposed to disappear?" I asked. "Tibet?"

He gritted his teeth and nodded.

"You were the one monitoring my movements in China. From California. Via Bill, via Dick. No wonder I had the feeling that I was being followed. It was you, wasn't it Freddie, making sure I didn't catch up with her. Making sure I thought I was closing the gap between us. Little by little."

Freddie drained his glass and stared at it.

I drummed my fingers on the table. "It was *you*, wasn't it?"

He nodded.

"But it wasn't Sally at all, was it?"

Freddie shook his head slowly.

"Who was it? Suzanne?"

"Damn," he whispered between his teeth. "Damn."

"But Suzanne never went to Tibet, did she? Bought the ticket in Chengdu and never got on the plane. Never intended to. Came back to Hong Kong instead. As planned." I sipped my gin and tonic. "Tell me, why did she impersonate Sally in China?"

"Why? Haven't you put that together?"

"Tell me about it," I growled.

"Not much to tell. It was a last minute decision. I didn't even know about it 'til the wheels were all in motion. I would have nixed it. Too dangerous. No reason to let a third party in on things to that extent."

"You thought Sally was going to pull her disappearing act in person?"

"Of course!" Freddie paused and looked me straight in the eye for the second time. "*I* did, didn't I?"

"What made her change her mind?"

"Sal didn't want to go into China in the first place. She was insistent. Not her kind of action."

"Understatement of the decade."

"And Suzanne looks a lot like her. But with dark hair. And she's an old hand at traveling. Suzanne's been working on boats and bumming around the world since she was sixteen."

"So Sally had a second passport made as a brunette."

"I didn't know about that 'til I got here," Freddie admitted. "What could I say? What could Suzanne say?"

"No?"

"No. Nobody says no to Sal's brilliant schemes. She was going to have Suzanne do it so she could just relax. And risk nothing. Wait for me, play on the yacht."

"With Marc."

Freddie finished his drink. "Strictly business."

"Want to bet?"

"I'd bet my bottom dollar!"

"I'll bet you already have. Listen, Freddie, what if I can prove that Sally has been lying to you all along? Just like—"

"No. No way."

"Just like she lied to Bill Barrett. You may have plotted larceny and adultery and income tax evasion, but my guess is that she and Marc have *much* more in store for you." I paused. "They used to be lovers."

Freddie jerked to attention. "Bullshit!"

"And no doubt still are."

"Oh, come off it! You can prove *that*?"

"No, but you can. And only you. One thing I can prove, though, is that Marc got Sally pregnant, and she had an abortion."

Freddie's eyes circled the ceiling with the fan.

"Given that," I went on, "her chance reunion with him via *Cruising World* seems highly improbable, don't you think?"

His eyes continued to circle the ceiling.

"If it was all a performance for you, like it was for Bill, what do you think the final act might be?" I paused again to shift gears. "What did you do with your Krugerrands, Freddie?"

"Krugerrands?" he repeated.

"You might as well tell me everything, you know. It's all going to surface anyway. And you're going to need my help, too."

"I cashed out my Ks," he finally confessed. "In Tijuana. Bought cashier's checks in Los Angeles."

"Deposited them in Hong Kong in a joint numbered account?"

He nodded.

"Tell me about the yacht."

Freddie fingered the photo of Marc and Suzanne. "Worth half a million. Free and clear. Sally and I gave fractional ownership to Marc and Suzanne, for port purposes. They're signed on as crew. They'll work for it."

I let his use of the future tense pass. "There's another half a million earning interest?"

"More like three hundred and fifty thousand. I couldn't leave GG in the street." Freddie glanced at my near-empty glass and held up two fingers to the waitress. "We were going to switch it to Vienna eventually. Get an account there that we could write checks on in any currency. Anywhere around the world. You know, pump up a local account with it."

"What if something were to happen to you? Would it all go to Sally?"

"Of course."

"What if something happened to both of you?"

"Who cares?"

"I care."

"Well, there was no point putting GG's name on anything, obviously. Or Bill Barrett's."

"That leaves the French connection, doesn't it?"

"Yes," Freddie answered solemnly, "it does."

The waitress brushed past the rubber plant. Put her thumb in one empty glass, two fingers in the other, clinked them together and lifted them onto a tray. Then sat two fresh drinks on the table. "'At's the spirit, luv," she told us.

"There's another dimension to all this," I said when we were alone again. "I want to hear about Sally's connection to Carole Oliver's murder."

Freddie gave me a blank look. If he was acting, he deserved an Oscar. "No connection," he said. "None."

"Carole was drowned in the Barrett's pool," I ventured. "The night before Bill returned from New York. Which leaves him innocent."

"Sally's innocent, too," he said.

"Let's hear about it."

Freddie took a deep breath. "I was with her that evening. We went to a film."

"And you took her home?"

"No. We met at the Nuart theater. Her idea, not mine."

"With Bill gone, why not take advantage of a rendezvous on Crestview Lane?" I asked. "Like you did on Saturdays, when you were off and Bill was working."

Freddie's eyes took on a peculiar mirror-like quality. I could see reflections of the potted plant in them. Finally he said, "That's what I thought."

"Could it be that Sally didn't want you in the house for a special reason?" I asked. "Like someone else was there?"

"But Sally's innocent. I know it. Time of Carole's death was in the middle of the film."

"Did Sally leave the theater at any time?"

"Absolutely not."

Somehow I believed him. "Did you know that Marc was in California at the time?"

"No he wasn't. He was in Hong Kong. We'd already bought the yacht."

I decided another fat lie wouldn't hurt. Besides, maybe it wasn't a lie. "Marc rented a car in Los Angeles," I said. "Same time Carole Oliver and Manuel Mandariaga were murdered." I tasted my fresh drink and gave Freddie a moment to process my questionable information before I said, "There's something very fishy here, and it isn't your squirming sack of prawns."

"Maybe," he said guardedly.

"The show's already over, but arresting you would let Sally off easily and Marc and Suzanne off scot free. And my guess is that they're the guiltiest of all." I stopped to give Freddie another moment to realize why.

"Listen, Freddie, you're going to have to trust me completely. If my suspicions are wrong, you'll have lost nothing. But if I'm right...well, I'm sure you can figure that out. Tell me what the next move is."

He made more wet rings on the table with his glass before he answered with a hoarse, "We're getting ready to haul out."

"When?"

"Next Sunday. After the Halloween Party."

"Party? Where?"

"On the yacht. A real blowout. Sal's invited half the club. Chinese lanterns, caterers, costumes, the works."

"Costumes?" I repeated. "Don't tell me. Like last year's?"

He nodded.

"And then?"

"Out the Balintang Channel. Skirt the Phillipines. To the Marianas. Micronesia. Tahiti. You name it."

"I will. It's called Down Under."

Freddie cracked his knuckles. "You mean Australia?"

I saw panic flicker in his eyes. "No," I answered gently. "That's not what I mean."

I looked up at the fan, wondering what was so spellbinding about it for Freddie. "Are you with me?" I asked.

He answered with a mechanical, "What's the game plan?"

"We'll take a taxi into Kowloon. Do some shopping at Sangso Electronics. You could be back here in little over an hour."

"Shopping?"

"I want you to plant some small recording devices around the yacht. We need to know what they talk about when you're not around. What's the schedule for tomorrow?"

"Thursday? Nothing specific. We're basically laying in supplies, going over charts."

"Then make excuses to leave for a few hours in the morning. Be gone 'til lunch. Any problem there?"

"I can tell them I'll get fresh fish here at the wet market. Roam around Sai Kung."

"That's the idea. And after lunch, can you make some excuse to go into Hong Kong?"

Freddie thought a moment. "I've been talking about picking up some spare parts for our Sat Nav equipment—Satellite Navigation—at the Ship's Chandlery. Near the Landmark Building. None of them has seemed interested."

"I'm staying right across the harbor. Peninsula Hotel. Room eight sixty-six. I'll be waiting for you there between three and four."

Freddie looked me with what I took to be sincere concern and said, "But what if Marc and Suzanne, or Sally, should find out that you're here in Hong Kong and not Tibet? That you picked up on the scheme? That would make *you* the number one target."

"If anything should happen to me, Freddie, it would be your doing. I doubt that you'd want that on your concience."

"No." Freddie fingered the photo of Marc and Suzanne again. "Guess I don't have much choice, do I? I suppose you've got all four of us under surveillance."

One more lie wouldn't hurt. "You got that right."

I took another sip of my gin and tonic to give myself time to think. There was a public phone on the wall near the front door. And no one sitting near it. "I'll be back in a minute," I said to Freddie.

I sauntered over to the phone and made what I hoped looked like a laid-back call. To Marine Police. I imagined Captain Yee pulling relentlessly on an ear as I filled him in on Freddie Grimm.

Chapter Twenty

I replaced the phone in its creamy cradle and lay back on the bed. Dick had just told me that Marc Sancerre rented a Nissan Sentra from National Car Rental in Los Angeles. He picked it up two days before Bill Barrett left for New York and turned it in the day after Bill returned home. I was in the middle of a giant sigh of relief when the phone rang again. It was Mr. Peng.

"Mrs. Taylor? You have a gentleman to see you here in reception. A Mr. Fred Graves. He says he's forgotten your room number."

I said, "Please send him up."

When I opened the door moments later, a limp Freddie Grimm stood in the corridor with a what-am-I-doing-here? expression on his face.

"Come in," I told him. "You're right on schedule."

Freddie managed a faint smile and a "Trick or Treat!" as he handed me a small plastic bag.

"Please make yourself comfortable." I motioned him to the chaise longue by the windows. "Something to drink?"

"*Anything* to drink." I could feel his eyes trailing me to the mini-bar on the far side of the queensize bed.

"Bourbon? Scotch?" I asked.

"Bourbon's fine." He flopped onto the chaise. "Lots of ice and a mist of water, if you don't mind."

I dropped ice cubes into two tall glasses, poured the Jack Daniels straight from the bottle, added a splash of water. I handed one to Freddie. "Cheers, luv," I said in East London brogue.

"Cheers, yourself!" He managed a nervous chuckle and clinked glasses.

I asked, "Anything new to tell me?"

"Not really. Sal did seem happy I was taking off today, though. Or maybe I'm imagining it. But I never had that feeling before."

"We often feel only what we want to feel, don't we." I drew a recording machine the size of a cigarette pack from my purse and placed it on the coffee table.

"Before you start that would you mind telling me how the hell you ever figured out that it wasn't Sally in China? It's been driving me up the wall!"

"Try a negative hypothesis marinated in garlic."

Freddie grunted. "By the way, the guy tailing me today was so obvious I could smell his breath.

"I run a tight watch."

"I'll just bet you do."

"And the less you know about that, the better."

Freddie gulped his bourbon. "You know, I can't imagine how a classy woman like you could enjoy traveling around in anything but style. How could you even *do* it?"

"Life divides people into two categories, Freddie. Tourists and travelers. Tourists never really leave home." That, apparently, gave him something to think about. "Now," I added, "let's hear the tapes."

Freddie watched me take the Octopus microcassettes out of the plastic bag. "Pretty neat gadgets, with their little suction cups," he said. "Stick 'em anywhere. Under a table. A bed. Even got one on the back of the helm. Nothing to it."

"Given the short time left before your scheduled departure, I'd bet on some major dialogue here. Especially when you weren't around. Like this morning?"

"From about nine to noon."

I held up a cassette. "G?"

"I marked them. G for the galley-salon, D for on deck, W for wheelhouse. F is for our aft cabin, M for Marc and Suzanne's. But mornings no one hangs around the cabins much. Or the wheelhouse."

"Then we'll try those three tapes first. This machine is sound-activated. If there's nothing but silence, it'll read them through in a few minutes. If there's anything happening, it'll give us a beep, stop and play."

All five tapes of the evening were a major disappointment. There was nothing at all out of the ordinary. Small talk. Television programs we fast-forwarded through. Freddie was squinting like Dirty Harry. I found myself humming "Look what they've done to my song, ma." Over and over.

The cabin tapes for morning revealed nothing but feet shuffling, a drawer closing, a toilet flushing, a soprano voice singing a few bars of *Madame Butterfly*. The wheelhouse tape contained little more than occasional footsteps and a faint voice that said, "I think he meant the Landmark Building."

I looked up at Freddie. He was fondling his glass of bourbon.

"Suzanne," he said.

I put in the deck tape. I was humming again. "It's turnin' out all wrong, ma. Look what they've done to my song."

The deck tape began with a trio of voices and sunbather banter. A few remarks about the possibilities of living in the Canary Islands for awhile. Then Freddie's voice announced, "Be back around noon."

I recognized Marc's heavy-cream French accent in the voice that said, "Pick me up a carton of Marlboros, will you sport?"

The machine zipped through several minutes of silence. Then the conversation resumed with a discussion of the danger of pirates around the Philippine coastline.

"Pirates?" I pressed the STOP button. Dick, a black patch over one eye, flickered for an instant on my inner screen.

Freddie got serious. "Oh, it's no joke around here. They're a plague. Even attack freighters. Come up over the stern at night. Mostly it's yachts, though. Usually they just want the electronic equipment, for resale. But we're armed to the teeth."

"What kind of arms?"

"Arsenal you wouldn't believe."

"Try me."

"Pistols, shotguns, bazookas. Two rifles with grenade launchers. A pedestal-mounted machine gun with a thousand rounds. What we locals call the 'Southern Cruising Kit of Arms.'"

"On board now?"

"No. Well...not all of it. Just some of the smaller stuff. Customs is supposed to confiscate everything. Hold it while you're in port, deliver it when you put out to sea."

"Nothing like good news." I pushed the START button.

Sally's now familiar voice said, "Freddie's such an asshole!"

Freddie put his glass down on the coffee table and hunched over it. Began cracking his knuckles.

"I don't know how I put up with him for so long," Sally went on. "I'm glad he's getting unstuck and poking around Sai Kung on his own for a change."

"Anybody want coffee?" Marc asked.

There were sounds of bodies getting up from the deck, comments about cappuccino, and a woman's sneeze followed by Marc's blessing, "*Dieu te bénisse.*" The remainder was blank. I pushed in the G tape.

The first two and a half recorded hours revealed nothing of interest. But the final half hour began with footsteps and what sounded like a coffee pot being set on the stove. The first words were unintelligible. "Whole story" was all I could make out. Then Sally's laughter, verging on hysteria. "Actually believed that I got you out of *Cruising World!*" she screeched.

"True only figuratively," was Marc's saucy rejoinder.

Freddie exploded. "That sonofabitch!"

I pushed STOP.

"And I trusted him! Sal probably—"

"Let's let *her* tell us, Freddie." I pushed START.

"Croissants?" It was Suzanne's voice. "I'll warm them."

"I'm in the mood for something sweeter," Sally cooed. "'I'm in the mood for love,'" she warbled. Freddie winced. "Let's open a bottle of champagne, shall we, Marc? Forget the cappuccino?"

A refrigerator door slammed.

"*Chéri*, would you do the honors?" Sally asked. "Lets celebrate! All those years, when we thought we'd never make it." Her voice had drained into a dramatic whisper. "All the waiting days...the loneliness...despair. With Baudelaire's black flag of melancholy nearly planted in our skulls. Remember? When you wrote me the poem? '*Le drapeau noir de la mélancolie.*'" The sound of a cork popping punctuated the end of her quote. "But we made it. We held onto the dream. And now we're living it."

"Almost," said Marc.

"Almost," Sally agreed.

Glasses clinked.

"Suzanne, did you change the order on the cake?" Sally wanted to know then.

"I did."

"I mean, can you imagine Freddie telling them to write 'HAPPY ANNIVERSARY, SWEETHEART' on it?" Sally's hysterical laughter rang out again.

"Don't worry," Suzanne reassured her, "I spelled out 'HELLO AND FAREWELL' for them."

"Let's drink to that, Sally," Marc said. "You too, Suzanne. 'Hello and Farewell.'"

I pushed STOP. "What's all this?"

"The Halloween Party cake." Freddie's voice sounded forced through a hollow reed. "It was our second anniversary. Sal wanted it to be hello to the good life and farewell to the past."

"I'll bet she did."

"What do you mean?"

"Let's see what I mean." I punched START.

"Put the croissants on the table, Suzanne. And find the papaya jelly, will you? Freddie said he bought some the other day." Sally paused. "And as for you, my Crash Gordon, come hither and give your waiting extraterrestrial a kiss."

"*Oui, ma capitaine.*"

Laughter mingled with assorted gurgles. I looked at Freddie and stopped the tape. His face had caught fire.

"I can't handle this." He erupted off the chaise, began to pace the room. "I'll kill him!" He kicked the bed, punched his right fist into his left palm. "I'll kick his ass up between his eyebrows!"

"Easy," I said gently.

"Christ, I work all these years looking into people's rotten mouths. Get GG all day long, GG every night. A total vanilla life! And then along comes this dream. No, don't tell me it's all a hoax. Don't tell me it's Sal—"

"*Sally* is telling you, not I," I interrupted. "Here, let me fix you another drink." I took his glass from the coffee table, crossed to the mini-bar.

"How could she do this to me?" Freddie sank down on the bed, put his head in his hands.

"You pass for a pretty nice guy. But *you* did it to GG. It's easy, isn't it? Just hard to swallow when you're on the receiving end."

I handed him a fresh Jack Daniels, sat down at the table and pushed START.

"Oh, Suzanne, bring a dab of butter, too," Sally ordered. "These are a tad dry." Then her voice melted. "'If it takes forever,'" she sang, "'I will wait for you.' Sing it in French for me, chéri."

"'*Non, je ne pourrais jamais vivre sans toi*—'Enough?"

"You're deliciously off key, but I *adore* it. Tell me again. How long before we get to Polynesia? I'm going to wrap myself in a Tahitian grass skirt," Sally burbled. "Deck my hair with plumeria. I will be *irresistible*! And we'll even find a nice island boy for our favorite cook here."

Freddie was livid. "How do you expect me to sit here and listen to her laugh at me?"

I punched STOP. "I wouldn't have handled the case this way if I hadn't believed in you. Believed you could keep both oars in the water."

A bent old man got up from the bed. "Easy for you to say," he mumbled, shuffling back to the chaise. "I loved her. I sacrificed everything I had."

"Including GG?"

"Everything I had. I did it all for Sally."

"For Sally? Wasn't it for you? For Freddie Grimm?"

He stared at me, then through me.

"Listen, Freddie. There has to be more to this story. Much more." I pushed START.

"Pour us champagne, will you, Suzanne?" Sally's voice-of-authority called out again, then mellowed with: "Oh, when I think of the South Seas, Marc. Gauguin dreamland. Skies full of stars. You and I—"

"Once we get Freddie out of the way."

"Well, there has to be a trade-off on this little stage."

"And the time is coming for the final act," Marc finished her thought. "By this time next week Freddie will have a real burial at sea at last."

"Poor little Freddie!" said a wistful Sally. "He's an okay guy. I really didn't mean him any harm. But he had to be expendable. Ridiculous Bill Barrett, too. What fools these machos be! Who the hell do they think they are? Think I'm for sale? Think they can buy me a bauble now and then and own me?"

I twitched at what sounded like the shreik of a peacock. Then Sally said, "Sorry Freddie, but somebody's got to lose the game, or nobody wins."

"And nobody's going to drag the Balintang Channel," chuckled Marc. "Even if he weren't supposedly dead already it would look like a simple accident at sea. Pirates—"

"Nasty pirates," interrupted Suzanne.

"Nasty, nasty pirates." Sally's laughter verged on hysteria again. "Pirates got poor little Freddie! God knows where they've taken him!"

I punched the STOP button. "Certainly not to Penzance," I said softly. Freddie's face was an empty theater. His eyes a dark stage. "It's worse than someone you love dying of natural causes, isn't it...the brutal death of a relationship. You have no love memory to guide you through the dark hours, to carry you across the abyss."

"You don't know what it's like."

"You might be surprised. We all want to edit our stories, Freddie. Rework the characters, shift the blame, massage the rage. Whatever it takes to salvage the illusion."

"Trash it."

"The only way to survive this mess is to accept it. The brutality of it. Understand the *real* Sally Barrett. And the real *you*, too. And then you can get on with your life." I went over to Freddie and put my hand on his shoulder. "You'll make it," I told him quietly. "I did."

Tears began to trickle down the rock walls of his face. Then, in slow motion, his head and shoulders crumpled into his lap. His sobs were almost inaudible.

I looked out the window in silence. A Turkish proverb echoed in my mind. "Before you love," it warned, "learn to run through snow, leaving no footprint."

Chapter Twenty-One

The following afternoon I left Hau Fook & Sons Tailors on Carnarvon Road and decided to walk back to the Peninsula Hotel. It was only a few minutes after four, and Freddie wasn't due until five. It would give me time to review my game plan—what Pat would term my textual strategies. If for Dick all the world's a stage, and for me a mystery, for Pat it's a text. This she describes as a system of narrative transformations. Most of her chatter about metaphysics and metalanguage flies right over my head without even considering a stopover.

Pat had sounded exhilarated on the phone earlier. The conference was over, and I guessed that her paper had been a success. She said she had five days before she had to be back at UCLA and jumped at my invitation to meet me in Hong Kong. She would cable her time of arrival tomorrow—Halloween.

I had also phoned Dick in the Palisades. He told me that Lieutenant Bashore had lost no time in locating the rental car Marc had driven and checked it out for signs of chlorine. There were still traces in the trunk. Bashore was now impatient to hear from me. Metropolitan's Agent Brandt, too. I told Dick to keep them on hold, and to make sure that Bill and GG accompanied him to Hong Kong. But they were not to know where they were going until they got to the airport. I made it clear that under no circumstance should he tell anyone that I had found Sally, or that Freddie was alive. Any additional party-crashers could ruin the performance.

Dick seemed to be perfectly willing to miss his Gilbert and Sullivan audition for a chance to play a far more thrilling pirate role on a real floating stage. He, too, would cable his time of arrival tomorrow.

"Travel light," I cautioned him, knowing his propensity for elaborate wardrobes. "Hauling clothes to Hong Kong is like carting owls to Athens."

Next, I'd had a lengthy planning session in Captain Yee's office. The Halloween party would be our one and only chance to lay traps for spontaneous confessions, and police support would need to be adequate. I was impressed with the three lieutenants he had chosen to work with us, especially with Sergeant Rob Scott, a delightful Australian expatriate who had been posing as a security officer at Club Marina Cove ever since I discovered Freddie in Sai Kung. Posted in the booth at the entrance to the piers, Scott would be the key guard on duty tomorrow evening.

The club's management had been cooperative from the beginning. At my suggestion, Captain Yee had led them to believe that a fairly small sailboat, with an orange and white striped lateen sail, was en route to Hong Kong from Macao, and that Marine Police had reason to suspect that it was planning to pick up a shipment of heroin from a junk somewhere at sea, then berth the vessel at Club Marina Cove. The story had facilitated the replacement of the regular security guards without arousing anyone's suspicions.

Whatever surfaced on the tapes Freddie was bringing at five o'clock would not alter the basic plan. Every move had been worked out in meticulous detail. We would leave from the Peninsula in two unmarked cars. In one, Captain Yee, a lieutenant, GG, Pat and I. In the second car, Dick, Bill, and the other two lieutenants. Three plainclothes officers would already be on duty in and near the clubhouse, just as they had been for the past three days.

Once on board, Captain Yee himself would stay close to Marc. The three lieutenants would pair off with Sally,

Suzanne, and Freddie. Dick would stand by GG in case of any emergency, while Pat and I would keep a close watch on Bill.

From the Marine Police office I had gone shopping. Costumes proved to be no problem in Tsim Sha Tsui. What wasn't already available could be sewn together in a matter of hours. It would all be delivered to my room by nine o'clock tonight. By then Freddie and I would have heard the tapes. Perhaps the dialogue for the final act would have materialized.

I turned left onto Nathan Road, and ten minutes later stood at the reception desk of the Peninsula Hotel.

Mr. Peng's froggy eyes were dancing around in their sockets. "Your reservations are confirmed," he told me. "Three single rooms for tomorrow night. May I have the parties' names, please?"

"Dr. Towne, Dr. Barrett, Mrs. Grimm and Mr. Kessler," I replied. Then added, "Dr. Towne will be sharing my room."

Mr. Peng fed the information into the computer. I could see that "Doctor" meant male to him. I would let Pat's appearance make his day. Mr. Peng then handed me two yellow and maroon checkered envelopes, each containing a telegram. I opened them immediately and read:

"Arrive Air France eleven thirty-five tomorrow morning. *Moi.*"

"Arriving thirty-first with Bill and GG. Thai Air at one forty-five. Bob Redford."

I smiled. Perfect, I thought. All the players will be on stage.

○

As I stepped out of the shower, I found myself singing the theme from *The Umbrellas of Cherbourg*. I pulled on a baggy pair of chocolate cotton pants and a peach and cream silk shirt that I had picked up at Hau Fook & Sons. I was pushing the sleeves up to the elbows when there was a timid knock at the door.

I opened it to: "Remember me?"

"Fred Graves, I believe." I took the small brown paper bag Freddie offered. "Come in."

"Nearly took a temper tantrum to pry Sal off the yacht today," he told me.

"Let me guess. You insisted that she had been ignoring you, that she didn't love you anymore. But if she did, she could prove it by having a romantic luncheon at the French restaurant in Stanley. And she couldn't say no."

"She could argue, though. 'Why go all the way to Stanley when we could go practically next door to the Surf Hotel?' she says. 'They have an excellent menu,' and so on and so forth. But I won. We left Club Marina Cove about ten this morning, got back around four. Then, as you also suggested, I pretended to have left my prescription sunglasses in the restaurant, and I was going to race back there to retrieve them." Freddie paused. "But then, since you no doubt had us followed, you already know that."

I shrugged and headed for the recorder on the coffee table. "So we have about six hours of tape? Excellent. Given what I suspect Marc and Suzanne have planned for the near future, I would think the subject would surface here. Why don't you help yourself to a drink while I load this machine?"

"Thanks, I will." Freddie started for the mini-bar, then stopped and turned around. "You know something? I think Sal was only too happy to see me leave!"

Two hours later Freddie and I sat staring at each other in silence. The script was complete. I picked up the phone and dialed Captain Yee's office.

"He left half an hour ago," Sargeant Suyin said. "You can reach him at home, though. You have the number?"

"Yes, thanks."

I redialed and Yee answered.

"Paige Taylor calling. I need to see you immediately. We have a new development in the case. You'll want to hear the second set of tapes Dr. Grimm brought me this afternoon."

"Can you come to my home?" he asked. "My wife and I would be pleased if you joined us for supper."

"I'd love to."

"Take a taxi to the Hopewell Center. I'll meet you out front. Our apartment is a bit hard to find."

"I'm on my way."

O

The next morning I was awake at the crack of dawn. Still satisfied from Mrs. Yee's dinner of sweet and sour ribs, I ordered only a pot of espresso from room service. Then I tried reading the *Hong Kong Standard* which came with it, but couldn't concentrate.

At eight I phoned Air France. Flight 801 from Paris was to arrive on schedule. I decided to do the rest of my waiting at Kai Tak. I showered and stepped into a pleated-sleeve dress in ivory crepe de chine—part of my new wardrobe from Hau Fook & Sons. I tucked *The Bourne Supremacy* into my purse and headed for the airport.

At the Air France desk there was other news. Flight 801 would be delayed for two hours, not expected to arrive now until one-thirty. I found a quiet seat where I could keep an eye on the ramp that led up into customs and opened the Ludlum novel. I was only on page seventy-eight. Dick was going to be disappointed.

"Alexander Conklin," I read. "Number one on Jason Bourne's hit list."

"Hit list," I murmured, and stared off into space. Infinity was getting closer.

I replaced the novel in my purse and pulled out my gold Cross pen and a spiral notebook. On the first page I printed and underlined FOOL ME ONCE. On the next I wrote:

"In a purple rage, Sally Barrett (née Leona Sally Romanski) stormed into the Pacific Palisades dental offices of Grimm and Barrett."

I would worry about changing the names later.

By the time my watch told me it was one-thirty and passengers from Flight 801 from Paris were beginning to trickle through from customs, I had finished a rough draft of The Prologue. By that time, too, the thought of seeing Pat had started butterflies fluttering in my stomach. My knees felt so weak, I decided I'd better stand and test them.

A moment later Pat made her appearance in a persimmon jumpsuit at the top of the ramp, shoving a luggage cart with wheels partial to circular movements. She caught sight of me coming towards her and rushed to say hello. The cart, abandoned to its own idiosyncrasies, bore down on us as we embraced. I had just enough time to gasp as it veered left six feet away and crashed into the wall, sending its two Gucci suitcases flying.

"*Merde!*" Pat told everyone around.

At that moment, Dick, Bill and GG burst through the door from customs. Dick, grinning from ear to ear, was maneuvering a more agreeable cart piled high with their luggage. Bill sprang to rescue the Gucci bags, and threw Pat and me a puzzled look. We had our arms wrapped around each other, like we were never letting go. Hadn't he guessed?

Then there were hellos all around, followed by my brief explanation of the situation to GG and Bill. "I know it was difficult for you, but I had to ask Dick to wait until you were at the airport to tell you that I had found both Sally and Freddie

in Hong Kong. I couldn't gamble on any information inno-
cently seeping out to Bashore or Brandt. Let's get to the hotel
and give you four time to catch your breath. Then I'll fill in
the gaps. Tonight should be spectacular, and you're going to
have to know your lines."

Pat arched an eyebrow. "Who do you think we are? Four
characters in search of an author?"

"It just so happens that we're going to a Halloween party,"
I announced.

"A Halloween party?" GG repeated with a lady-of-the-ca-
mellias smile that was straight from the final act.

"You'll make it," I told her quietly. I looked at Bill's glassy
eyes. "You will, too."

Bill deflected his emotions with, "By the way, how's the
tooth?"

"Not bothering me at all," I replied.

"The rear molar, huh? Well, not to worry. Even if it takes
a root canal, you won't feel a thing. A little shot of Carbocaine
and...let's have a look."

I shuddered. "Later," I told him firmly.

"That's the trouble," Bill went on. "It's that damned
plaque. Those colonies of bacteria that get to living down in
there and, well, if you'll pardon my French," he added,
turning to Pat, "it's like they're going to the toilet on your
teeth."

"What a lovely image," noted Pat.

I took her arm with one hand, GG's with the other. "Let's
get a taxi," I said.

Chapter Twenty-Two

When our alarm clock buzzed at four-thirty that afternoon, Pat and I reluctantly uncoiled and rolled out of a queen-size bed that now looked like a leftover from Tropical Storm Zebra.

"What do you say we meet here again?" I asked her. "Say around midnight?"

"Same bed, same skin?" she giggled. "You're on."

We showered and lost no time getting into the party clothes I had ordered for us. The floor-to-ceiling mirror in Room eight sixty-six of the Peninsula Hotel soon reflected my face framed in the cowl of an Aegean-blue cloak that fell to my ankles. Next to me Pat was vogueing about in one of the oddest dresses she had ever worn. The shimmering silk shoulder-to-ankle sheath that matched her radiant green eyes was slit up the sides to above the knee. The glittering silver brocade piece that fit to the front of it was curved in the shape of a dagger. Its jeweled handle of turquoise and jade was clasped over Pat's heart, its tip gathered over her right thigh.

"How do we look?" I asked.

"Too obvious," answered Pat.

There was a sharp knock at the door. "We'll add the Lone Ranger masks later," I said, and crossed the room to open it.

In the hall stood Bill Barrett in a frog suit that turned even his eyes reptilian. GG was clad in early Cinderella, with a dirty blond wig and a spangled mask that made her features indiscernible, and Dick looked like a swashbuckling dream. Black leather pants tucked into black leather boots, a red and white striped shirt with bandanna to match, a black patch over one eye, and a silver pirate pistol in each hand. He took one look at my cloak and Pat's dagger and groaned.

"I couldn't resist," I told him, then turned to GG and Bill. "Captain Yee and crew should be outside by now. Remember, when we get to the marina, say nothing but what we've rehearsed. Hopefully, your presence will add emotion to the scene at the right moment, and to the spilling of truth. But any giveaway ahead of time would spoil the whole plot." They both looked at me with eyes full of fear and heartbreak. "I know," I added, "it will take all the strength you have."

GG nodded. "Yessum," she said.

"Croak, croak," came from the frog's mouth.

Downstairs, I handed all four keys to Mr. Peng. He leaned against the wall, listing so far to starboard that I thought he would capsize with a faint breeze. I could feel his glossy eyes trailing our quintet across the lobby.

Two unmarked police cars were waiting outside. In them were Captain Yee and his three lieutenants in handsome Marine Police uniforms—rich navy blue with gold trim.

Fifty minutes later both cars pulled into the parking lot at Club Marina Cove. Lightning cracked the southern sky, followed by a distant rumble. Beneath it Pat and I and the four officers transformed ourselves into a tipsy sextet in matching black masks. We led the way past the clubhouse to where Sergeant Rob Scott was checking identification at the security guard booth on the pier.

"What 'ave we 'ere now?" he asked Captain Yee in his meaty Australian accent.

"Four Marine Police officers," Yee replied sternly.

"Aw, don't come the raw prawn wi' me, mate," the sergeant laughed, waving us on.

Over the top of her mask Pat arched an eyebrow at me. "Come the raw prawn?"

"Aussie for don't pull my leg."

The six of us stumbled ahead. Bill plodded along slowly several paces back; far behind him trailed Dick and GG, hand in hand. Where the central pier divided, our unsteady squad swayed left down a narrower plank pier. Its slips were filled with sailboats that reminded me of the smart ads in *Cruising World.*

Long before we could see the party yacht, we could hear its music. I recognized Verdi's *Un Ballo in Maschera.* How apropos, I thought, an opera seething with rage and anguish and adulterous passions, complete with sailor and sorceress, conspirators, traitors, and plots of murder—plus a tragic dénouement at a Masked Ball.

Just beyond the black and tan cruiser CARAMBA, the swank motorsailer HERE LIES THE HEART loomed into view. The name was prominent in gold bas-relief on a sleek white hull. The deck, strung with Chinese lanterns, was a ferment of party animals.

With Captain Yee on one arm and a lieutenant on the other, I staggered up the gangplank. Pat, shrieking with laughter, dragged behind, leaning heavily on the other two officers.

"Welcome aboard!" a black-tighted Hamlet told us as he gave me a hand.

"Trick or treat!" I said.

"Plenty of treats below," the familiar voice answered.

"Take me to the nearissht bar," demanded Pat, "before these characters arresht me!" She gave the officers a playful shove.

Hamlet bowed. "Follow me."

"Never could remember what ya call the front and the rear of a boat," Pat went on with a five-martini giggle. "All I know's that there's a *sssharp* end and a *bluuunt* end."

Hamlet led all six of us around to the blunt end, past Attila the Hun, The Thief of Baghdad, two anorexic fairies, and a reclining creature whose T-shirt read Lizard of Oz. We moved on through the wheelhouse and down a short stairway into the galley.

It was candle-lit and smoky. Two bartenders in red devil costumes were busy fixing drinks for a pair of Siamese twins—joined at the elbows—labeled Alpha and Omega. A waiter in seedy drag headed topside with a heavy tray of Chinese Dim Sum. Pat snitched a wonton as he passed by.

I was happy to note that most of the guests chose to remain outside. That would certainly simplify things. If it didn't happen by chance, assembling the essential parties below decks would not be difficult.

In the salon adjoining the galley, next to the stereo, stood a leggy, blonde Cinderella-at-the-Ball. She was in the middle of an open-throttle soprano aria. "'*Che ti resta, perduto l'amor*—'" she sang, along with Kiri Te Kanawa, lamenting that her love must die, wondering what is left once love is dead.

Yes, Sally, I thought. What *is* left?

"'*Non tradirme*,'" Cinderella trilled, then stopped abruptly. Her eyes were fixed on the stairwell. I didn't need to turn my head to know that a frog had appeared. It plopped awkwardly through the galley and across the salon, stopped at the margarita fountain on the dining table and helped itself to a drink.

"Croak," it said to silent Cinderella.

She recovered from the ghostly image with a burst of laughter and finished her aria with a crusty "'*Mio povero cuor!*'"

Applause accompanied her as she strutted over to the flipper-clapping frog. "And who might this foolish creature be?" she asked playfully.

"Croak! Croak, croak!"

"Croak yourself!" screeched Cinderella. "And welcome to the party, you funny frog!"

Welcome to reality, Bill, I said to myself.

Bonnie and Clyde appeared in the passageway leading to the fore staterooms. I recognized them from the photo Pat had sent. Bonnie, now awash in necklaces, flounced into the center of the salon in a beaded flapper dress with watermelon cloche hat and mask to match. A dainty pearl gun handle protruded from the holster-shaped purse that dangled from her wrist. Clyde followed, dapper in a brown pinstriped suit, fudge shirt, tie and spats. When he curled his thumbs around his watermelon suspenders, two inside shoulder holsters bulged into view. They looked like .357 Magnums to me. I hoped Freddie was right—that none of the guns would be loaded.

While the opera raged on, Cinderella headed for the wheelhouse door, arm in arm with Bonnie and Clyde. Perfect timing, I was thinking, as a grisly howl came from the stairwell. Into everyone's view burst a Gilbert and Sullivan pirate with a tattered waif in his arms.

"I got one whale of a thirst," he roared in an accent I placed somewhere between Campy-Southern and Serbo-Croatian. "An' ahm a-gonna drink mah full!" He brushed A Great White Hunter out of his way en route to the margarita fountain. Pat and I exchanged arched eyebrows.

Cinderella's eyes darted from the frog to the waif. Once. Twice. Then to Hamlet. He shrugged nonchalantly and edged towards the stereo.

"I'll bet you're the Rigolots on that neat little ship *Dream Time*, right?" a recovering Cinderella asked the pirate. "In the slip just across from us?"

"Yes, Maam. We shore are."

Shore?

Cinderella looked down at the waif. "Came in yesterday? From Sydney?"

"Yessum," came a whispered sound from the tatters.

"Well, welcome to the party!"

The time had come. I nodded discreetly to Hamlet. He turned the volume down on the stereo, pushed STOP, EJECT, and removed the cassette of the opera.

"Hey!" An irritated Cinderella stopped in the wheelhouse doorway, steered Bonnie and Clyde back into the salon.

"Ladies and gentlemen," Hamlet shouted above the chatter, "may I have your attention, please?"

"What now?" I heard Cinderella murmur to Clyde.

"Attention, please!" Hamlet shouted, then nodded to the trio in the doorway. "Won't you all take a seat?"

The chatter dissipated. A bewildered Bonnie and Clyde sat down on the loveseat by the margarita fountain, flanked by a standing Captain Yee and a Marine Police lieutenant. Another officer leaned against the wall behind Hamlet, and the fourth wobbled onto a bar stool next to Cinderella. The pirate moved to the entranceway with his arm around his drooping waif. Pat and I remained by the starboard portholes, next to the frog.

"I have here an original tape recording," Hamlet announced. "I'm sure you'll find it quite fascinating." He inserted the new cassette and punched PLAY.

"Alone at last, *mon amour, mon petit* Crash Gordon," a mock soprano voice began. "Come love your little Sal."

A man answered with a heavy-cream French accent: "Let me make sure they are really gone."

Footsteps were followed by a short silence, then footsteps returning.

"Gone, *chérie!*" the man said. There was a pause, then: "Ummmm."

"What kind of a farce is this?" Cinderella's eyes narrowed as they traveled from Bonnie and Clyde to Hamlet. "If this is your idea of a joke, Freddie—"

"Ummmm," the smoky female voice went on, "hold me."

Bonnie and Clyde lurched to their feet. "Turn that off, Freddie," Clyde told Hamlet.

Hamlet punched OFF. He looked at the stony Cinderella by the bar. "We haven't heard the best part yet," he told her.

"We did it just for a lark, Sal," Bonnie stammered. "It was all Freddie's idea!"

"Bad joke, Sal," Clyde agreed. "It was supposed to be a funny little skit." He turned to Hamlet. "Let's end it right here, Freddie."

"What do *you* say, Sal?"

Cinderella moved to the center of the salon. "We'll hear the tape, Freddie," she told him in a voice like frozen tundra. "*Now*."

The red devils, the Great White Hunter, Alpha and Omega, and the half dozen other guests froze. With their blank, puzzled eyes, they momentarily reminded me of the cartload of pigs I had seen in Kunming.

Hamlet pushed START.

"Just think," the woman's alto voice continued in French, "next week we'll be lying in the master suite, in that delicious kingsize bed, with ummmmmm—"

"Goddammit, I said turn that off, Freddie!" Clyde headed for the stereo and Hamlet.

Cinderella moved in between them. Her "Leave it alone, Marc" reverberated around the room like a death rattle.

"Ummmm," the male voice overlapped. "As soon as we get rid of Freddie. Then Sally."

"Man and woman overboard!" the woman cried out.

"Hello and farewell!" said the man. "*Bonjour et adieu*."

Hamlet punched STOP, folded his arms. No one moved.

With the ear-splitting shriek of an enraged peacock, Cinderella threw herself at Clyde. He caught her wrists just as her red-laquered nails reached his throat. Suddenly all the spectators in the room looked as if they belonged in Madame Tussaud's Wax Museum.

A Chinese man in a white baker's suit emerged from the stairwell and crossed the galley into the salon. He was carrying a large rectangular cake. On the white frosting were bouquets of blood-red roses and the words "HELLO AND FAREWELL." His eyes flickered nervously around the room. "Where you want this?" he asked.

"You can put it on the bar," Hamlet told him. "We're rehearsing a play," he added, as Cinderella and Clyde writhed about the center of the salon. She was coiled around him like the serpent around Laocoön.

The baker nearly threw the cake on the bar, backed out of the room and hurried up the stairs. By then, Cinderella's screams were liquifying. "Marc, tell me! Tell me it's not true! Tellmetellmetellme!"

Hamlet took a step towards her. "That's what you planned for me, Sal, isn't it?" he rasped. "I have all that on tape, too. 'Man overboard!'" His voice was imitation Cinderella. "'Those nasty pirates got poor Freddie!' Somewhere in the Balintang Channel, huh?"

"So now you know," Cinderella hissed at Hamlet.

"And now you know, too, you bitch! *Salope!*" came from Bonnie, as all the bitter, tangled emotions of the waiting woman rose to the surface. "Off!" she screamed. "Get your hands off my man!" Bonnie landed a solid kick on her rival's left shin, eliciting another ear-splitting shriek.

Clyde jerked Cinderella a safe distance away from his moll. "You wanted the money, didn't you?" he snarled. "You'd do anything for the money, you said. The hell with Freddie. And that fool Bill Barrett. They didn't matter, did they? Well, you didn't matter either. Is that so hard to understand? I didn't give a fuck about you either."

Cinderella slumped against Clyde. The moan that rose from the dead center of her being sent shivers up and down my spine.

"I was going to have your baby, Marc." Her voice was in slow motion now, her words pushed out in uneven intervals. "Your baby! Don't you know what I went through for you? I lost my family for you. And you never loved me?"

"I loved you once." The steel surface of Clyde's voice began to bend. "That first spring. That first summer. And then I met Suzie. But you clung to me like a crab. Got your claws into me and wouldn't let go."

"You wanted to get rid of me?" Cinderella broke into hysterical laughter.

Clyde's steel voice snapped back into place. "Why not?"

"Yes, why not?" Bonnie repeated. "You had your fling. All those little rendezvous with Marc. Two weeks alone with my husband while you had me traipsing around all those stinking places in China."

Cinderella stared at her. "Husband?" she breathed.

"Yes!" hissed Bonnie. "*My* husband! *Mine!* Paris last winter. California in August. But little did you know that I was always there. That Marc went to you from *my* arms. And it was *my* arms he came back to."

"August," Hamlet repeated. "You were both at the Barrett house when Carole Oliver came for Bill's keys that night, weren't you? Carole caught you in the act, didn't she?"

"That's not true, Marc," whispered Cinderella. "Suzanne wasn't there with you."

"You bet I was," said Bonnie. "We made love right in your back yard." It was Bonnie's turn to laugh. "In your own back yard!"

"And your gig would have been over with Sally if you hadn't killed Carole," Hamlet went on. "So you drowned her in the pool, dumped her in the ocean. My compliments to you both. It was fast thinking, fast work, and you got away with it. Too bad the old guy next door saw you. But you knocked him off, too, didn't you? Pretty impressive."

"They got in our way," said Clyde, and with that gave Cinderella a shove towards Hamlet. "So you win, Freddie. You get Sal. You two can just sail off into the sunset."

"I don't want Sal," said Hamlet. He went over to the pirate's waif and gently removed her mask. The face that appeared was awash in tears. He said, "I'll make it up to you, GG."

Cinderella gasped. "So you were in on this, too?" She looked over her shoulder at the frog. "Oh, my God!" she stammered. "It's you, Bill, isn't it."

Bill Barrett removed his frog head. Beneath it was a glassy-eyed ghost in a spotted green suit.

That did it. Cinderella turned into a whirling dervish, hurling anything within reach. Glasses, bottles, dishes, trays. Their contents sprayed the room, spattered the guests. Shattered glass showered the floor like silver confetti. I could feel my nerves beginning to fray.

Clyde took a long look at Bill and GG, then grabbed Bonnie by the arm. "Come on, Suzie. We're outta here." They zigzagged across the salon like a pair of star quarterbacks.

Hamlet leaped between them and the stairwell. "It's not that simple," he told them. "You're not going anywhere."

I held my breath. This was the moment of truth.

Clyde's "Move it!" boomed out of him like God telling the First Couple it was time to exit from Eden.

"Not on your life," was Hamlet's solemn reply.

Bonnie and Clyde reached for their guns. The four Marine Police officers drew their own.

"Drop those," commanded Captain Yee.

The matched pair let their pistols slip back into their holsters. They froze into a final pose, like the last frame in a film.

"You three are all under arrest." Yee's nod included Cinderella. "For murder and conspiracy to commit murder, among other things." He turned to Hamlet. "You'll have to come with us, too."

"Alas, poor Yorick!" Pat whispered in my ear.

"And all of you present here may be called upon as witnesses," Yee continued. "You will please register with my officers before you leave this vessel."

Pat took the frog's limp arm. "Come on, Bill," she said. "Let's get some air." She steered him through the galley and on up the stairs. The look in his eyes told me the teenager was gone.

Across the room, a silent Cinderella stared at a handcuffed Clyde. Topside, someone began to sing *The Party's Over*.

Epilogue

The tropical storm that broke over Sai Kung shortly after midnight had hooked north, leaving nothing in its wake but an intermittent drizzle. Singapore Air's Flight 306 to Honolulu and Los Angeles lifted off the Kai Tak runway right on schedule. By the time I was ushering Pat and Dick into a taxi outside the airport, the 747 should have sliced through the cloud cover and leveled off at forty-two thousand feet in a bright blue sky. Bill and GG should soon be unbuckling their seat belts and directing their thoughts to the cocktail hour.

I settled into the rear seat of the taxi next to Pat and Dick and gave the driver directions to Wyndham Street on Hong Kong Island. Once through the Harbour Tunnel we followed Gloucester Road towards Central, and not far from the Landmark Building our taxi swerved to the curb. Pat looked out the window at the unpretentious sign over a doorway. I read her lips: "Jimmy's Kitchen?"

"Sergeant Rob Scott's suggestion," I told her. "That we try Australian oysters on the halfshell here. And their steak and kidney pie. He called it a *gweilo* hangout. That's Chinese for *gringo*."

I paid the driver and we scampered through a sprinkle of rain into the restaurant.

It had the quiet clubby elegance of an expensive British pub and eatery anywhere in the world. Thick carpets, pewter mugs and platters, solid dark furniture—that English veneer that the creators of such establishments carry about with them like tortoises their carapace. No matter where they stop, it is still and always England.

We chose a circular table in a corner near the bar. I ordered a bottle of Piper-Heidsieck from a tuxedoed giant with gull eyes, fish lips and a generic smile. He soon had three bubbly flutes set before us, and the remainder of the bottle retaining its chill in a silver bucket nearby.

I clinked glasses with Pat and Dick. "To you," I said. "Without you, this case would literally have run aground, and Sally Barrett and Freddie Grimm would be at the bottom of the Balintang Channel today."

Dick said, "So much for dreaming of a stiff breeze to Java."

"And winding up with a high wind in the nasal passages," was Pat's comment.

"She's speaking in tongues again," murmured Dick.

"I'm glad GG isn't pressing charges," I said. "With a little help from Metropolitan Life and the D.A., Freddie should be released from custody here soon. He was wrong about only one thing. Those *loaded* Magnums! Lucky we didn't have a booming display of fireworks to end the party."

Pat rolled her eyes. "To think that the spacey guests topside took it all as part of the entertainment, like some implausible melodrama blaring out of the speakers up on deck. There they were, applauding their hostess in handcuffs, expecting Captain Yee to pass out prizes for best costumes!"

"So what's to become of Sally now?" Dick wondered. "Extradition to start with, right?"

I nodded. "According to Yee, jurisdiction should be California. Sally will probably get off fairly easily, compared with Marc and Suzanne. But I doubt very much that she'll ever plot murder again. My guess is that she'll settle for a simpler life."

"Let's hear it for downward mobility," said Pat.

"I still can't figure out why Sally was so damned hooked on Marc in the first place," Dick put in. "If you ask me, Freddie's a hell of a lot more attractive."

"Guilt is thicker than blood," was Pat's reaction. "Remember Leona Romanski? The nice Polish Catholic girl from Cicero?"

I nodded again. "Fitful first love and a frightful abortion. That's a scar that lasts forever. But Sally romanticized her story and called it eternal love."

"Symbiotic mush," Pat put in. "More like obsessive attachment."

"Like nostalgia for a Never Was," I said, remembering my evening in Stanley. "Illusion. There's the real killer."

"Just ask Madame Bovary," added Pat.

"Well, so much for Sally." Dick swung an invisible gavel and landed it on the table. "But murder one for Marc and Suzanne!" Dick's eyebrows took on the peculiar Iago slant that he picked up in a Shakespeare seminar last spring. "Picture that August evening," he went on. "Carole Oliver reaches for Bill's keys. Hears a pair of lovers by the pool. Carole can't wait to frame Sally and latch on to Bill. So she climbs over the gate. Finds herself face to face with our future Bonnie and Clyde. They lure Carole in...." Dick's eyes fluttered upwards in what I suppose he meant to be some sort of simulated drowning scene.

"Poor Manuel Mandariaga," I said. "If he was at the shrine, he was tall enough to have seen it all over the fence."

Dick nodded. "The fingerprints Lieutenant Bashore got from the murder weapon should soon meet their match."

The three of us fell silent, thinking of the cast-iron Madonna. I finally turned to Pat and said, "I'd like to invite Silvia and Elena to dinner when we get back."

"Let's. I'll whip up a paella."

"And as for you, my love, I hope this entire scenario will at least inspire another erudite paper for your academia nuts to chew on. Some new critique of logocentric presencing perhaps?"

"How about *The Hermeneutics of Disguise: Representation and the Cosmos in—*"

"Amen!" Dick bowed his head. "I think that must be my subtle clue to exit this stage. I'm off to Wan Chai," he announced. "To leave you two to your oysters and kidney pie."

"Looking for someone to lift your celibacy?" teased Pat.

Dick twitched his mustache and finished his champagne. "So you two are jetfoiling it to some romantic hideaway in Macao tomorrow while I get to write a couple dozen marinas letters of apology on *Nautilus* stationery."

"And why not wire Marc's mother some flowers from Pat? A little thank you. Some to Alyce Maine, too. For her 'Get Keys' contribution. Also, please see to it that the champagne I ordered for Mr. Peng is delivered."

"Check."

"While you're at it, don't forget to have a few suits made at Hau Fook & Sons. Put it on my bill."

"Thanks. I'll do that."

"But stay away from the Pussy Cat Bar," I told Dick as he prepared to leave. "And Ricky and Pinky's Tattoo Parlour."

"Check again," he said with a wink. "See you at Kai Tak day after tomorrow." With that, he was gone.

The tuxedoed giant reappeared and refilled our flutes. "Here's to my sweet Paige." Pat raised her glass. "I imagine this tale will inspire another novel. How about telling me what you're going to call it? What's the material for a novel anyway, but something to accompany a telling title?"

"That's hardly like you, Professor Towne," I said. "I would have expected something like...a way of mapping, tracking, and taming the heterogeneity of the universe."

Pat gave me an eyeroll. "Now who's speaking in tongues?"

"Something has to have rubbed off on me in this relationship."

"I'll let that one pass. At least until we get back to the room."

I raised my glass. "Until then."

Other Books from Madwoman Press

On the Road Again
The Further Adventures of Ramsey Sears
by Elizabeth Dean
Irreverent magazine columnist Ramsey Sears tours America, finding adventure and romance along the way. This is the critically acclaimed sequel to *As the Road Curves*.
$9.95   ISBN 0-9630822-0-5

That's Ms. Bulldyke to you, Charlie!
by Jane Caminos
Hilarious collection of single-panel cartoons that capture lesbian life in full. From dyke teenagers and lipstick lesbians to the highly-assimilated and the politically correct. This Lambda Book Award finalist is a must read.
"These funny cartoons depict moments in lesbian life with a fine edge." —Women Library Workers
$8.95   ISBN 0-9630822-1-3

Lesbians in the Military Speak Out
by Winni S. Webber
Women from every branch of the armed forces tell their stories about being women and lesbians in the military.
"It documents voices previously silenced by legal and social censure . . . highly recommended reading amidst the confusing and often painful dialogue . . . concerning the role of gay and lesbian people in a democratic society." —Minerva Quarterly Report
$9.95   ISBN 0-9630822-3-X

Thin Fire
by Nanci Little
Elen McNally signs up for a three-year hitch in the Army, thinking it will get her a one-way ticket out of Aroostook County, Maine. A remarkable coming of age story. Nominated for an American Library Association Gay and Lesbian Book Award.
". . . compelling . . ." —Lambda Book Report.
$9.95   ISBN 0-9630822-4-8

Sinister Paradise
by Becky Bohan
A professor of classics finds herself endangered by an international

arms-smuggling conspiracy just as she finally finds love. This fast-paced adventure is set amidst spectacular scenery in the Mediterranean. Bohan weaves a tight drama.

"... a riveting tale of love and greed in a country of olives and deep blue water." —Minneapolis Star Tribune
$9.95   ISBN 0-9630822-2-1

Mrs. Porter's Letter
by Vicki P. McConnell
Nyla Wade, recently divorced and starting a new career as a reporter, discovers a packet of passionate love letters buried deep within the old desk she's just bought. Her journalist's curiosity piqued, she wonders if the writers, W. Stone and Mrs. Porter are still alive and embarks on a search to find out. First book in the Nyla Wade mystery series.
$9.95   ISBN 0-9630822-6-4

The Burnton Widows
by Vicki P. McConnell
Lesbian journalist Nyla Wade arrives in the costal community of Burnton, Oregon to start a new job and discovers a limestone castle, old murders and a town anxious to forget both. Nyla's unwanted probing re-opens old wounds, unleashes local gay activists and uncovers the truth about what happened the night of the murders. Second book in the series.
$10.95   ISBN 0-9630822-7-2

Double Daughter
by Vicki P. McConnell
Nyla Wade goes home to Denver for a visit and finds clouds of menace hanging over the lives of friends, old and new. Although the threats appear to be the work of a well organized anti-gay groups, Nyla suspects the source is closer to home. Soon she's the next target! Third book in the series.
$9.95   ISBN 0-9630822-5-6

□   □   □

Madwoman Press welcomes orders from individuals who have limited access to stores carrying our titles. Send direct orders to Madwoman Press, Inc., P.O. Box 690, Northboro, MA 01532-0690. Please include $2.50 for shipping and handling of the first book ordered and $.50 for each additional book. Massachusetts residents please add 5% sales tax. A free catalog is available upon request.